# Christmas
# GRIFFIN

# Christmas
# GRIFFIN

MARIE CARDNO
WRITING AS
ZOE CHANT

# I

# DELPHINE

Delphine Belgrave was completely fucked. At least, she hoped she was.

She squinted through the windscreen. She'd spent enough time in the States that driving on the right-hand side of the road wasn't a problem, but there was barely enough road here to *have* a right-hand side. And it was pitch dark, threatening snow, in the middle of the mountains.

For the last two hours the GPS on her phone had assured her she was going in the right direction. Then she'd accidentally bumped it while reaching for her water bottle, and when she picked it up she realized with a sort of expectant horror that although the app had indeed been meticulously tracing her car's progress along the winding mountain roads, the roads on the map were not the roads she was actually on.

Expectant horror, because the way this vacation was going, she'd been expecting something else to go wrong any minute.

"Oh, good," she'd breathed, like she was worried about upsetting her phone's feelings. She tapped at the screen, trying to reset the map, and discovered she had precisely zero signal. And zero GPS. Were those different things? That was the sort of question she'd usually Google, probably to pre-empt her boss saying something stupid, but her boss was thousands of miles away on a mindfulness retreat and she was here in the mountains on the family holiday from hell and she had to face facts.

She was lost.

Stuck in the mountains in the middle of the night, who knew how many miles away from the quaint tourist village of Pine Valley where her entire extended family was gathered to celebrate Christmas.

It was the best news she'd had all week.

Oh, it would cause some problems, certainly. But she hadn't volunteered to go and find a liquor store in the neighboring county because she wanted to spend every holly jolly minute of the holiday with her family. Oh, sure, she would have to make up some story—perhaps she could say that traffic was so bad that she hadn't been able to make it to the nearest city to pick up a bottle of her grandfather's favorite port wine and back in the same day, and had stayed overnight.

She couldn't tell the truth. If she told her family that she'd driven back into the mountains, port safely stowed in the back seat, and merely gotten lost, then they would wonder why she hadn't simply shifted into her winged lion form and flown up to look for the glow of the town lights.

The answer was that she couldn't.

Delphine Belgrave came from a long line of winged lion shifters. Her younger twin brothers were winged lions, her late father had been one, and his father before him, and the family history stretched back further than even her Aunt Grizelda could trace. All lions, all the time.

Except for her.

Delphine came from a long line of shifters and that was the phrase she used, usually, when someone asked. It dodged neatly around the fact that she wasn't one herself, and she made sure never to put herself into a situation where she was expected to transform, or use telepathy, or display any of the other magical powers shifters had. Faster healing, better resilience and enhanced senses were all gifts of a family heritage she had entirely missed out on.

She'd become an expert at faking it over the years.

Now, not even her own family suspected she was a break in the Belgrave shifter family tree.

And she intended it to stay that way. Which was why she'd done everything she could to miss the most recent family get-togethers. Her job as PA to a self-centered, high-flying pegasus shifter was a great excuse. Family birthdays? She would have to video call in; Mr. Petrakis was attending a conference. Reunions? She wished she could, but she had to prep for an emergency meeting with key clients. Christmas? *Such* a shame, but Mr. P needed her to manage his schedule, and his accommodations, and make sure the fridges were stocked with the latest brand of sparkling water he'd become convinced would re-align his chakras, or whatever he was believing this week.

Technically, that last one hadn't been a lie this year. Mr. Petrakis wasn't in the mountain town of Pine Valley somewhere in the frozen bit of the United States… yet. He was much further south, in a desert, learning mindfulness. Or possibly doing a variety of drugs. The brochure for the retreat had been very unclear.

Which should have left Delphine with a precious week to herself, soaking in Pine Valley's cozily American Christmas atmosphere a whole ocean away from her family, and drinking mulled wine and eggnog until it ran in her veins.

Except then she'd driven into town and discovered every shop, restaurant and grocery store full of Belgraves, and all her plans had been pulled out of her hands like the last mince pie on Christmas Day.

She could handle it. She *could*. She was a Belgrave, after all, even if she hadn't come out right. And the first way she was handling it was by leaving town—temporarily. Her grandfather, the patriarch of the Belgrave clan, had insisted that someone find him something to drink that was more palatable than the dross available in Pine Valley's stores. Delphine had jumped at the chance. She always did. It made her feel a bit like Cinderella, doing everyone's odd jobs and errands, but it got her out of the way. And this latest errand was an absolute winner. Spending a whole night away without worrying that someone was trying to speak to her telepathically or would insist she join them for a sneaky midnight flight…

Bliss.

She would wait until it was light, take her time getting her bearings, and slowly make her way back to Pine Valley. If she timed it right, she would miss family breakfast and perhaps even lunch as well. And she would pretend, as she always did, that the opportunity to get herself out of a fix by using shifter abilities had never arisen.

*If only they hadn't come at all*—She pushed the thought away before it could take root. No point wishing for things that hadn't happened or for things hadn't happened that already had.

One night down, she told herself. After that, four to go. Tomorrow, then Christmas Eve. After that, the big day—she couldn't exactly skip out on Christmas, but hopefully everyone would be so sozzled on food and drink that they wouldn't notice anything out of the ordinary about her. One more day after that, for everyone to sleep off their hangovers, and then the great Belgrave clan would go their separate ways. Most of them would fly directly back to the UK, where they were all lived.

Five nights. Delphine closed her eyes. Five nights. Four days—four and a half, if she counted the final day, when everyone would be packing and leaving.

She could manage that.

She had better.

Because if she wasn't very, very careful, then the lies she'd built up around herself over the last fifteen years would come crumbling down before Christmas was over.

She checked the time. It was past nine; if her GPS hadn't failed her, she would have almost reached Pine Valley by now. Night seemed closer out here in the mountains. Darkness pressed against the side windows, and even the headlights seemed thin and weak, as though the night was too powerful for them. If she turned the car engine off…

Click.

Complete darkness. For a second, her eyes didn't want to catch on; after-images of the light inside and outside the car lingered in her vision. She blinked them away and stared out at the full pitch black.

It was as though the world was completely empty, and she was utterly alone.

Something that had been knotted inside her for so long she'd forgotten it was there slowly released.

"It's beautiful," she whispered, but that wasn't enough to describe the feeling that filled her at the sight of all that nothing outside. It made her wish that—that—

She let out a hard, heavy breath and wrapped her arms around herself. Forget what she wished; she'd just found a little problem with her big plan to stay in her car overnight. With the car's heating turned off, the darkness wasn't the only thing pressing in.

Turned out, winter in the mountains was cold. Who'd have thought?

Delphine grimaced at herself and turned the key. The car roared back to life: engine, heating, defog all back on. The night's enchanting emptiness faded away, replaced by a sight more troubling than Grandmother Elaine peering at the hotel's wine list.

Tiny flecks of snow were dancing in the beams from her headlights. As she watched, some of them landed on the windshield and melted. Then bigger flakes joined them, flurrying more heavily through the air, and when these ones landed, they didn't melt.

"Oh, good," Delphine said again. It wasn't like there was any point in saying *oh, bad*. She knew it was bad. Saying it out loud wasn't going to change that.

Night was one thing. She could explain away staying out of town overnight. Snow? Oh no. If she got snowed in here, it'd be all *Why didn't you dig the car out yourself?* and *Why didn't you take wing when the snow started?*

Of course, that was a relatively best-case scenario. Worst case, she froze to death out here. She didn't want to even imagine her relatives' reaction to that.

*What sort of a Belgrave freezes to death?*

She straightened her shoulders. "I didn't think you'd appreciate port slushies," she murmured, rehearsing what she might say to her grandfather later. "You can't think I'd have *chosen* to drive back, in these conditions?"

That was barely even a lie. It was hardly *choosing* when the alternative was three generations of Belgraves tutting over her pathetic human corpse.

She got out her phone again and compared the real map to the incorrect one from earlier, and her hazy recollection of the turns she'd taken. Biting back a sigh over the certainty that a real Belgrave would have perfect recollection, she tried to figure out where she *actually* was.

*If only—*

She shook her head sharply. There was no time for *if onlys*, here or in the rest of her life.

How would she manage this if she were comparing the map against, say, her boss's directions? She wouldn't trust Mr. Petrakis's memory, for a start. She would assume he'd gotten himself turned around at least once, and that whenever the GPS instructions and the road in front of him hadn't matched up, he would have taken the closest option and blamed the map for being wrong...

...Which wasn't too different to what she had done herself, she realized. The GPS had sometimes told her to turn left where no left turn existed, or continue straight off the edge of a cliff, and she'd mentally edited the instructions: waiting for the *next* left, no matter how much further along it was, and so on.

Which, if she was figuring this right, meant that she was somewhere around...

The middle of nowhere.

"Oh good—" she began and cut herself off with an irritated huff. It was obvious to anyone that the situation wasn't *good*. And it wasn't as though there was anyone around she had to impress.

It wasn't the *utter* middle of nowhere. Just deeper into the mountains than she had expected. She'd somehow managed to miss Pine Valley entirely. But it was only a few hours' drive away, if she was right about where she actually was. She might even make it back before midnight.

She didn't think the words 'time to slink back home with my non-existent tail between my legs,' but it was a near thing.

The car grumbled as she pulled onto the road again. First things first, she needed to turn around—but she couldn't do that here. She'd have to keep going and keep an eye out for a wider bit in the road, where she wasn't going to risk turning into a tree or snow-covered rocky outcrop as she tried to three-point-turn her way around.

The snow became thicker as the road climbed up the mountain. Once, when the trees opened up on the downhill side of the road, she thought she caught a glimpse of warm lights that might be Pine Valley. At least it was in the direction she'd decided Pine Valley was in, which she decided to take as reassuring.

Something like another light flickered through the trees above as she navigated a particularly sharp and narrow turn. A house, she wondered? Who would choose to stay this deep in the middle of nowhere? Even shifters, careful to keep their magical natures secret, would surely choose the warmth and camaraderie of a town filled with their kind over such solitude.

The car thudded over a hidden rock and she bit her lip, the light forgotten.

At no point did the road widen—if she'd come across another vehicle, after she'd died of shock she would have had a difficult time figuring out how they were meant to pass one another—but after a few more bends and another tempting glimpse of the glow of street lights far below, she found what looked like a stopping area on the side of the road. It was covered in pristine white snow, and she heaved a sigh of relief. The snow on the road itself had been getting deeper, and she didn't want to drive any further up the mountain than was necessary. If she got stuck…

She shook her head. She couldn't get stuck, because if she got stuck, she would have to be *rescued*, and then she would have to explain herself to her family, and everything would be ruined.

Delphine turned the wheel and backed onto the space. Snow crunched beneath the car, the crisp sound audible, even over the rumble of the engine. The car dipped slightly as it broke through the crust.

Then it dipped more.

Then it *fell*.

Delphine yelled as the car sank into what was not, after all, a pristine patch of perfectly flat ground perfect for turning around. It was, in fact, a ditch.

# 2

# HARDWICK

Hardwick Jameson always planned ahead. Which was why when he arrived in Pine Valley and, instead of the half-abandoned ghost town his friend and ex-colleague Jackson Gilles had sold him on, had found a bustling tourist village full to the brim of locals, visitors and—he shuddered at the memory—*Christmas cheer*, he had a back-up plan ready to go.

An old hunting cabin in the middle of nowhere. The perfect place to spend Christmas by himself.

He winced as he remembered the few minutes he'd spent in town before he turned his car around and drove further up the mountain. It had been an automatic response.

*A defensive response*, he corrected himself, and sighed. There was no point him being here if he was going to lie to himself. And even white lies hurt this time of the year. Papering over his problems by tempering his words wasn't going to help.

The hunting cabin was a rustic affair. The largest room acted as mixed kitchen, dining and lounge, with an ancient iron stove. To one side was a smaller bedroom and to the other, the bathroom and laundry. There was a smaller shack on the far side of the clearing, which he'd assumed was normally used for hanging meat, and had decided to use as an extra-cold storage during his stay.

He'd lit a fire in the large iron stove when he arrived and had been pleased to discover that it warmed the whole place well enough. He could have coped with the cold, but this trip wasn't meant to be some sort of tortuous penance. It was a retreat. Recovery.

Hardwick made himself a cup of instant coffee and sank down into the worn sofa. From here, he could have looked out the window to the small clearing around the cabin and, beyond that, the ring of trees just lit up by the light coming from the house.

Instead, he looked inside himself.

Hardwick was a griffin shifter. When he was in human form, his inner griffin lived in what Hardwick could only describe as his soul. Not that he would have described it that way to anyone, if anyone had asked. Lying was one thing, but some things were private.

His soul was the same as it had always been. He thought of it like a room inside his head. A nest, maybe. Reassuringly stable.

If he closed his eyes, he could see his griffin there. Some shifters could hear their inner animals, he knew, but his griffin was silent. It made its thoughts known through gestures—a sort of personal sign language, Hardwick called it. Gestures and feelings.

Mostly, the feeling was pain.

There was a reason Hardwick spent the end of each year alone. His griffin couldn't talk, but it didn't need to when it came to what it did best: sniffing out lies. Its senses were so finely attuned that it could tell when someone was lying from up to twenty feet. In the new year, when Hardwick returned to work refreshed, the lies would feel like a buzz at the back of his head, or a tight muscle in his neck. Now, at the ass-end of December? Each lie was like a hammer to his skull.

Right now, his griffin was still on edge. That didn't surprise him. Pine Valley had been a bad shock not only the number of people filling its streets, but the number of shifters. For shifters, living among humans meant almost constantly lying about what they were.

And it was Christmas. If there was a better time of year for people to lie to themselves and everyone around them, Hardwick didn't want to know about it.

Out here, though, he was far enough from even the most intrepid holidaymakers that nobody's lies could touch him. Total peace, for the first time in a year.

He closed his eyes and sent reassurance to the griffin. A week with nobody but himself for company and they'd be back in action.

His griffin twitched its claws. He felt a tingle in his eyes and opened them to let it peer out into the world.

"See?" He looked around the room slowly, then out the window, letting his griffin take in the beautiful serenity. "There's no one here but us. You can relax."

He took a sip of coffee and grimaced.

"No one here but us and worse coffee than we get in the station," he grumbled. His griffin clacked its beak in agreement and Hardwick relaxed.

They were going to be fine. Work. Retreat. Get well enough to work again and put his gift to good use. He had a system, and it hadn't failed him yet. These last few months had been harder than usual, but—this was going to work. It always did.

Without warning, pain shot through his skull.

"What the hell?" He jumped to his feet. Coffee spilled across the floor as his mug fell to the ground. Inside his head, his griffin was all fur and rustling feathers, defensively puffing itself up.

The pain was gone as quickly as it had arrived, but he didn't let that fool him. Someone else was here.

Hardwick swore to himself and barged over to the door. Icy wind whipped against his face as he slammed it open. Snow, too. The flakes were the size of his fingernails, deceptively soft as they flurried through the open door.

There was no sign of anyone outside.

He narrowed his eyes, drawing on his griffin's enhanced senses to see through the darkness more clearly. It strained inside him, its lie-sensing powers reaching out despite itself. *Like scratching an insect bite even though you know it'll make it hurt worse,* Hardwick thought, his stomach clenching.

Nothing. No sight, or sound, of anything in the darkness surrounding the cabin. No sign of whoever it was that threatened his much-needed solitude.

On a winter's night.

With snow deepening on the ground, and the air so cold it was biting the inside of his mouth.

Crap.

Hardwick ground his teeth. "Is someone out there?" he called. Then, using telepathic speech because given what Jackson had told him about this area, it was as good a bet that a shifter had gotten themselves into trouble on the mountain roads as a human: *Is someone out there?*

# 3

# DELPHINE

W as that a voice?

Delphine stopped moving. She willed her teeth to stop chattering and strained her ears until she couldn't hear anything over the blood pumping through them, but it didn't help. Compared to the rest of her family she might as well have been locked in a sound-insulated bubble.

She stumped back towards the car. The snow was coming down so fast it was settling in small drifts on her shoulders—she'd never seen anything like it.

She knew she should be worried that it was too cold, that the chill was slipping in the gaps between her hat and scarf, sticking icy fingers up her sleeves past where her gloves reached. But it wasn't the thought of what might happen to her that scared her. It was the thought of how her family would react when—

"You're being silly," she scolded herself, and repeated the words she'd been trying to reassure herself with ever since she crashed. "That's not going to happen. I'm going to get this car free—" *Somehow,* she added silently. "—and get back into town, and everything is going to be *fine.*"

Somehow.

She wrapped her arms around herself and looked over the car. It hadn't moved since the crash, unfortunately. Its back wheels were still deep in the snowy ditch and its front wheels just touching the edge of the road. If she got the chains out of the trunk and put something under the front wheels for them to grip on, maybe she'd be able to get enough purchase for the four-wheel-drive to pull out of the ditch.

She repeated the plan out loud to herself, pretending she was explaining it to her boss. There weren't any holes in it that she could see—at least none that her boss would have been able to see through.

Delphine bit her lip. A plan that her boss could not see any holes in was not necessarily a plan that had *no* holes in it. And now was not a great time for her to realize that she'd put so much effort into creating a Mr. Petrakis Worldview to guide her actions that she might have slightly lost track of how the real world worked.

In her defense, the plans she tested against the Mr. Petrakis Worldview were usually somewhat less potentially fatal than this one.

But driving in snowy or icy conditions were what chains were for, surely. She should have put them on the car before now, but she hadn't been expecting the fresh snow, and the last time she'd been in Pine Valley the locals had grumbled about visitors using chains around town and messing up the roads. And—

And in short, she thought, sighing, she could come up with any number of excuses for why she'd gotten herself into this situation, none of which were going to help her get out of it.

But she had a plan.

"Everything's going to be fine," she reassured herself. Saying it out loud made it feel more real. She straightened her shoulders. Normally, she wouldn't add this, but right now…

"It *will* be fine." Her voice was almost a growl, which surprised her. Determination stiffened her spine. "Because I'm a Belgrave, damn it. A *real* Belgrave. No piddly snowstorm is going to stop me."

Whether she believed the words or not, they helped. She leaned over the edge to open the driver's side door, and carefully placed her foot in the same safe hole-in-the-snow she'd used to clamber her way out.

And missed.

Her foot hit not a convenient rock, but a hole—one that got deeper the more of her leg was in it. She struggled to get her weight back onto the leg that was still on the road, but it was too late.

She swung around, pivoting on the door handle and the complete absence of solid ground under her foot. The door shut, and she slammed against the side of the car; one foot dropping into nothing, one dragging behind her on the road, and her grip on the car door handle slipping.

Her heart thudded uselessly in her throat.

She couldn't go down like this. God, how embarrassing. She just had to—to—

Not let go of the door handle.

As soon as the thought crossed her mind, her fingers slipped.

She toppled backwards. Something hit the back of her head, and everything went black.

The world fuzzed back into existence around her. Or maybe she was the fuzzy one.

*Please*, a part of herself that she thought she had gotten rid of long ago whispered. *Maybe this is it—maybe it's late, but I am a shifter after all.*

It did happen. It had happened last Christmas, right here, in Pine Valley. A man who had thought he was a normal human for the first twenty-something years of his life had suddenly discovered he was a shifter. Delphine was a twenty-something. And if there was ever a time for her inner lioness to show up, this was it.

She moved her limbs tentatively and all hope went out the window. Human arms, human legs. No wings. Worse, they were moving sluggishly. She half-felt as though they weren't her arms and legs at all.

"Damn it," she croaked out. "I can't die here. No real Belgrave would—would let a little thing like—"

Everything went black again.

The next thing she remembered was probably a dream. It could have been hours later, or seconds. She tried to move her arm. Something thudded against her side. It was dark: the same close, all-enveloping darkness that she'd breathed in so longingly before.

It didn't seem as welcoming now. Or perhaps it was too welcoming.

Her lips shaped the words she'd been trying to say before. "A real Belgrave wouldn't let this stop them," she whispered, not sure if she was speaking out loud or just imagining it. "And I'm a real Belgrave. I…"

Was that a sound? A voice? Delphine strained against the smothering blackness, the cold and heavy weight of the night. Something appeared above her. A face. Dark eyes, staring at her with an expression that—that—

She groaned as shadows crept in at the edges of her eyes and everything went black.

*Again.*

# 4

# HARDWICK

The world stopped spinning.

Hardwick moved by instinct. Long hours of training pushed him through motions his brain wasn't capable of processing. Check for injuries. Check for breathing.

Curse himself for not moving faster, for not thinking ahead and bringing a blanket, something warm, something to stop her body's warmth from seeping out like water through a colander. Curse himself for hesitating when he first sensed her presence. For those few resentful seconds he'd spent wondering what the hell anyone else was doing out here, where he was meant to be alone. For the minutes he'd spent getting dressed again once he landed down here in human form, as though his goddamn modesty was the important thing here.

Pick her up. Check airways again. Watch her eyelids flutter. Watch her not wake up.

Wonder how long she'd been out here.

Hardwick pulled his heavy jacket off and wrapped it around her. It wasn't much, but it would have to do. He laid her down carefully and shifted into griffin form. Snow cascaded around his wings. Some of it landed on the woman. He brushed it aside and carefully picked her up in his front claws. He felt like he was moving through tar.

He clutched the unconscious woman against his feathered chest and leapt into the air.

She was so still. A limp, heavy weight. He was acutely aware of the cold wind rushing past, the snow flurrying every thicker around him as he wheeled up towards the sheltered clearing where the hunting cabin was. Snow was already thick on the ground up here. His car was bumper-deep.

Her car had been more than half-buried. In a few hours, it would have been invisible. Wiped out by the fresh snow. She would have been—

He landed. Ripped the door open. Laid the woman on the sofa and shifted back into human form. Checked vitals. Breathing, pulse, all steady.

He remembered seeing an ancient hot water bottle in one of the cupboards and put water on the stove to heat. Blankets from the bed. Took off her boots and gloves, found feet and fingers cold but not ice-white. Blood still in them. Tucked the hot water bottle against her chest.

Found some clothes. Tucked himself against her chest, folding his body around hers, creating a pocket of warmth to protect her.

Slowly, horribly, the world started moving again. The numb shell that had surrounded Hardwick the moment he saw the woman lying helpless in the snow melted away. His griffin twitched and fretted, watching her out of his eyes.

She was a few years younger than he was, he guessed. It was hard to tell, with her face smoothed out by unconsciousness and gone pale with the cold. Her hair was honey-gold, darkened by patches of melting snow.

Questions there hadn't been time for during the emergency welled up, unstoppable.

Who was she?

Where had she come from?

And before he could stop it, a cracked, resentful voice added its own question. The voice that crept into his thoughts when his headaches were at their worst, and the whole world seemed fixed on hurting him.

Because this was no ordinary woman. He didn't know her, had never met her, but from the second he caught sight of her in the snow he'd understood on a level beyond ordinary senses who she was.

His soulmate.

And that broken voice inside him, the dark shadow of the man he wanted to be, whispered:

*Why did fate tie me to a mate whose lies are so powerful I could hear her from a mile away?*

# 5

# DELPHINE

Something smelled like smoke. Delphine's nose twitched. *Oh, good. Mr. Petrakis has left his curling tongs on again*, she thought, and without opening her eyes, sat up and swung her legs off the side of the daybed.

Something else moved, too, something that she barely had time to register as warm and solid before it disappeared. Her brain put two and two together and came up with *Oh, good, Mr. Petrakis has adopted another fashionable type of dog and set it on fire.* She tried to stand up.

Her feet hit something soft and unmoving. She kicked at it, confused, and found there was something wrapped around her legs. And her head hurt. And—

Everything that had happened rushed back to her.

No curling tongs.

No smoking Samoyed.

No daybed in the corner of her office, where she stole a few minutes' sleep after staying up all night managing Mr. Petrakis's latest disaster.

*Oh… good.* It was only long training with her family that stopped her from swearing out loud. Was she still in the snow? Did she feel like she had something wrapped around her legs because her legs were completely numb from the cold? Was she *dying?* Was this what dying felt like? Like being trapped somewhere while your boss absent-mindedly set fire to his office bathroom and your head was sore and everything smelled like burning and… coffee…

"You're awake."

The voice was like a calming landslide. It rolled over Delphine's sudden panic, flattening her wild thoughts so she could see them for the nonsense they were.

She opened her eyes.

She wasn't stuck in the snow, or back at the office sneaking a micro-nap before her boss burst in with his latest grand plan. She was inside a room she'd never seen before, lying on a sofa she didn't remember getting onto, wrapped in warm blankets.

The back of her head still hurt. She sat up—slowly, this time—and gingerly felt around the pain while she looked for the person who had spoken.

When she saw him, she went completely still.

Delphine believed in magic. Of course she did. She came from a family where people could transform into giant mythical beasts, for heaven's sake. Where people could speak telepathically and bounce back from minor injuries like they were nothing.

Where every person had a soulmate they recognized on sight.

The ache in her head suddenly felt a long way away. Delphine had the strange sensation of being detached from her own body. That wasn't unusual in itself—how many times had she felt like she was standing outside of herself and looking in, making sure she wasn't letting anything slip?

What was unusual was the sensation of standing outside of herself and looking at someone else. Because once she saw the man who'd spoken to her, she couldn't look away. Not even to make sure she was behaving correctly.

He was the most captivating person she'd ever seen. He looked—

Her eyes took him in greedily. He had dark hair and a hawklike nose beneath heavy, forbidding eyebrows and deep-set eyes; he was too far away and the light in the room wasn't strong enough for her to tell what color they were. He was cleanshaven, with a strong jawline and…

…and…

She couldn't look any further. Her eyes kept darting back to his. She felt as though she was searching for something. Like if she could just look at him for long enough, she would… she would…

She thudded back into her body with a gasp.

All at once, she was acutely aware of her breathing, her heartbeat, the sudden heat on her skin.

*Oh, God.*

She wished she didn't have a name for what she was feeling. Or that it had a different name. Shock. Post-almost-dying syndrome.

No.

*Love.*

It had to be. Because what was happening… was *exactly* what she'd always been told would happen.

Eyes locking across a room. Breath catching in her throat. Everything else in the world fading away until it was just him, and her. A sudden, joyful desire—and with it, certainty so clear it might have been carved into her heart.

She'd just found her soulmate.

So why did *falling in love* feel so much like utter horror and dread?

Delphine's lips were dry. She licked them, hunting through her own feelings. Where was the happiness? Where was the heart-deep joy, the contentment in knowing the rest of her life was sitting there in front of her?

Her brain was moving too slowly. She couldn't understand herself. Then she focused outward, on him—on her *mate*—and found the answer.

He didn't look as though he'd just stumbled upon the love of his life. His expression was neutral—no, it was *deliberately* neutral. Which meant it was actually wary, or watchful.

She knew that particular expression far too well to mistake it. It had taken most of her teenaged years to train herself out of it. Any Belgrave worth their salt could tell when an expression said too little.

Delphine's breath caught in her throat. She wasn't sure whether it was hope or fear that stuck it there. She wasn't sure of anything and she couldn't remember the last time her own responses had been so unfamiliar to her. She didn't know how to react. He wasn't giving her anything to bounce off of, and that meant all she was left with was her own confusion.

The man's eyes wrenched away from hers. It felt like someone had pulled her heart out through her chest.

"You're awake," he said. His voice was rough and went straight to a soft, vulnerable place inside her.

"Yes," she agreed. That was something she could be sure of, at least. Solid ground. Solid-ish, at least. "Where… am I?"

"At a cabin I'm renting for Christmas," he said. "Looked like you crashed your car. We're a fair ways from the nearest town."

He gestured towards a cell phone sitting on the kitchen counter. "I've been trying to reach someone in Pine Valley, but the call keeps cutting out. Weather's playing havoc with the connection."

*That's a relief.* Delphine let her eyes sink shut. Weather too bad to make a phone call meant weather too bad to fly in, surely. And if her poor map-reading was in any way accurate, then she was too far out of town for anyone to expect to be able to reach her telepathically.

"Why the look of relief?"

Delphine's eyes snapped open. "Don't be ridiculous," she said, smoothing the blankets. "I'm not relieved."

He grimaced. "You don't need to lie," he said. "So, you're not broken-hearted about missing Christmas. Big deal."

"What are you talking about?"

"Oh, forgive me. 'Cos when people drive halfway up a mountain in the middle of a snowstorm, they're usually *not* trying to avoid their families."

"I wasn't avoiding anything."

"Sure you weren't."

This was beginning to feel more like an interrogation than a rescue mission. "The only reason I was out today was to run an errand for one of my relatives."

"The *only* reason?"

Heat rushed to her cheeks. What the hell was his problem?

"Look, I'm grateful that you helped me, but I don't see how my reasons for being out here are any of your business." She forced herself to look into his eyes, not thinking there could be any danger in it.

That was a mistake.

Oh, God.

His eyes were so dark they pulled her in. Something fluttered in her chest. *Blood pressure problems following a stressful event,* she told herself, but she wasn't convincing anybody. Least of all the slow, languid heat that poured through her limbs. It was the complete opposite of the vigilant bundle of nerves she'd always thought of as her true self. And between them… a spark.

Her lips parted. Sitting in the armchair across from her, he looked just as stunned. He leaned forward. The deep line between his eyebrows eased. "Did you—"

A flicker. Something alive and curious looked out from behind his eyes. She knew at once that it wasn't him. It was something else: an inner animal, staring out even while he was in human form.

He was a shifter.

*Idiot.* This was why she never met anyone's eyes. Not for long enough for something like this to happen, anyway.

She tore her eyes away, before he could hunt in them and find nothing there.

She had to get this conversation back on track.

"How did you—" She didn't know how she was going to end the sentence. Find me? Know I was there? Get me back here? She shook her head, hoping it would knock loose some inspiration, and instead it throbbed. She hissed in a breath and put one hand to the back of her skull.

"Let me." The man stood up. Her stomach flip-flopped. He was *tall*. Not tall and broad, like the Belgraves, but not slender, either. He was lean and powerful, like the joy of flight given form.

He sat down beside her on the sofa and reached for the back of her neck. She tipped her head forward and held her hair out of the way. It was tangled and matted. Which wasn't worth feeling self-conscious about, but her cheeks heated up regardless.

"You weren't bleeding when I brought you in, but you have a lump. I'd guess you fell, hit something just hard enough to stun, and the cold did the rest." His fingers were gentle as he inspected the bruise and Delphine closed her eyes automatically. It almost didn't matter that it hurt, if he was touching her. "It's still swollen. I'll get you some ice."

She couldn't take it anymore. The tip-tilted feeling inside her, her uncertainty—it was too much.

Delphine twisted until she could look up into the man's face. This close, she could see the color of his eyes: so dark a brown they were almost black.

He hadn't moved his hand when she turned around. His fingers rested against her cheek.

She wanted to kiss him. She wanted to kiss him almost as much as she'd ever wanted anything.

And it was that *almost* that stopped her from doing it.

"What's your name?" she whispered.

He held her gaze. "Hardwick." His eyes flickered. "And yours?"

"Delphine Belgrave."

"I'd say it's a pleasure to meet you, but…"

Her brain itched. She glanced around the room, half-expecting to see one of her relatives lounging in a corner. The brain-itch was her one claim to any sort of shifter magic. She couldn't hear telepathic words, or talk to anyone else using only her mind, but when someone tried to talk to her mind-to-mind, she got a little, scratchy buzz in the back of her head. Like static from a T.V. in another room. But there was nobody here except her and the strange, watchful man.

*And that was definitely telepathy.* She turned back to the man, like a pendulum swinging back on course. If she'd had any doubts before—and her life was all doubts—this settled it. He must be a shifter. Which meant—

It meant that at last, she was on solid ground. This was something she knew how to handle.

She bit her lip. "You're a shifter, aren't you?"

His eyelid flickered in recognition. But he still wasn't giving anything else away.

That didn't matter. She had enough to go on.

She smiled. "Don't worry," she said. "Your secret's safe with me. All of us Belgraves are shifters, too."

# 6

# HARDWICK

Hardwick flinched.

The lie cracked against his temple like a fist. Delphine stared at him, cool and collected. No sign on her face that she'd just lied to him.

His griffin screeched unhappiness. He schooled his face to careful neutrality, turning his flinch into a natural pulling-away.

"That so?" he asked, mildly. He was asking for it, he knew, but—

"Yes," Delphine said, her English accent not giving anything away. "We're all winged lion shifters."

Ouch.

"I see."

She licked her lips—a sudden betrayal of nervousness, or another calculated move? Hardwick felt himself slipping into work mode. This woman, his *mate*, was lying to him. Why? What was she hiding?

His griffin hitched its wings, a small, anxious movement that gave away more than Hardwick wanted to admit to himself.

He answered its silent question.

*I know she's meant to be mine. But I can't—don't you feel that? It's like she's wrapped so many lies around herself that it hurts even when she's not talking.*

It clacked its beak softly.

*Of course I want to help her—just let me figure this out. I have to think—damn it!*

He stood up. Delphine's eyes stayed glued to his, and he turned away, unreasonably unsettled. "I'll get that ice," he muttered, and stalked away.

Icy wind tugged at his hair as he grabbed a tea towel and the pick from beside the front door and headed out to the out-building he was using as an extra freezer.

Whoever had last rented the place had the same idea; the block of ice he hacked chunks off looked like something out of *Little House on the Prairie*. Simpler than an ice machine, though.

He wrapped a few shards of ice in the towel and paused, staring back at the cabin.

He'd felt the moment his griffin recognized the woman as his mate. He'd felt it when he first saw her, face-down and unconscious in the snow. A cold hand had gripped his heart and not let go. Not when he raced to her side and found the pulse in her neck.

Not when she'd murmured half-formed words as he lifted her from the snow. Not when he'd brought her back up to the cabin and wrapped her in blankets, warm beside the fire, and found the lump on the back of her head.

Not even when she woke up.

He could see it now. Even with his eyes open, staring at the cabin, he could see the moment she'd woken up fully from the restless half-consciousness he'd found her in.

It was as though the sun had come down to Earth for a vacation. Her hair was honey-bright, her skin glowing with golden health as she lost the last of the snow's chill. Beneath expressive half-moon eyebrows a few shades darker than her hair, her eyes were a compelling mix of brown and sparkling citrine. And when she'd looked at him—

She was older than he'd initially guessed, he thought now. She'd looked younger when she was sleeping, and still for a moment after she woke up. Then something else had settled over her features. A sharpness that added age and exhaustion to her in a way that made his heart clench further under its icy coating.

He knew that look. He'd seen it enough times, on the other side of an interview room. It was the look of someone trying to twist a situation to their own benefit.

So, it didn't matter what he'd *felt*, when he was saving her life, or afterwards. It didn't matter that the icy fist around his heart had melted the moment her golden eyes met his. That his heart had reached out for her. Or that his griffin had unfurled its wings and raised its head, gazing at her without the same painful suspicion that he greeted all strangers with.

How naïve.

He ran through her lies in his head.

*All of us Belgraves are shifters, too.*

*We're all winged lion shifters.*

She was a Belgrave. No lie there. Which meant either Belgraves were some other sort of shifter than winged lions… or not all of them were.

She hadn't responded when he tried to communicate with her telepathically.

All this suggested that she was a non-shifter from a shifter family—but why lie about something like that? It happened. Sometimes shifters were born from non-shifter families, and sometimes non-shifters were born from shifter families. It might have something to do with genetics. He didn't know that anyone had done research into it. It was just one of those things that all shifters knew.

So why lie?

There had to be something more to it. And much as he wanted to find out why this woman wrapped herself in lies, much as he wanted to help her the way he dedicated his life to helping others, he didn't have time for *something more* right now. He needed rest. A total retreat.

He needed for his goddamned head not to hurt every time he looked into those golden, lying eyes.

He was still trying to make his head stop spinning when he got back inside and stomped the snow off his boots. Delphine was still sitting on the sofa. She'd gathered the blankets around herself like a cloak, and just for a moment before she turned to look at him, she seemed… worried.

Then she noticed he'd returned, and her face smoothed over. Except for that exhausted sharpness at the edges of her eyes and the tilt of her head.

"Ice," he said, and handed it to her. She pressed the bundle against her head with a sigh.

"Thank you." She gave a grateful smile. "I know it'll heal quick enough, but this helps the pain, at least."

This time, he managed to hide his wince of pain.

"Something to drink?"

"Oh—coffee, if you have it."

He thought of the poisonous cup he'd dropped earlier. "You might regret that. I've only got instant."

"I'm not that fussy. Instant's fine." A white lie. The sort of thing he could shrug off in January but stuck like a burr in December.

"Your funeral."

He filled the kettle again and set it on the always-on iron stove. There was only one spare mug on the counter. He cursed and scouted around the floor for the one he'd dropped. Delphine gave him a curious expression as he grabbed it and made a half-hearted attempt to mop up the spill.

She kept watching him as he spooned instant coffee into the mugs and waited for the water to boil. He didn't look back at her, but he was as sure of her eyes on him as he was of her restlessness as the silence lengthened.

"Thank you," she blurted out at last. "For s-saving my life. I didn't know there was anyone else out here. I thought—" She let out a heavy breath. "I don't know what I thought."

His griffin whined as the lie hit home. He snorted. *I don't need you to tell me that wasn't the truth.*

"Call it a Christmas miracle," he suggested, wondering what it was that she had thought in the moments before she fell into the snow.

"I suppose." Blankets rustled as she moved around. "I'm curious, actually. I know it sounds ungrateful, but I'm dying to know what you're doing all the way out here. At Christmas."

Four sentences, and not one of them was a lie. He was almost impressed.

The kettle whistled, and he poured water into the mugs. "Milk, sugar?"

"Yes to milk, no to sugar."

He fixed her drink, then hesitated, and decided to take his black. "Here."

"Thanks."

Her bright eyes tracked him as he sat down opposite her, in the same worn armchair he'd been in when she woke up.

He braced himself and took a sip of his coffee. Delphine did the same. Her eyes went distant and horrified. "Oh. Um. Yum," she said. It was so unconvincing a lie, he wondered why his griffin bothered to point it out.

But point it did. With claws.

Rubbing the pain in his temple, he put his cup down. "You wanted to know what I'm doing out here?"

"What can I say? Apparently, I'm the sort of person to look a Christmas miracle horse in the mouth. Or something."

"Griffin, not horse."

"Sorry?"

He leaned back. This mystery woman, his mate, deserved to know what she was dealing with.

And part of him wanted to see how she would react to the truth.

"Griffin," he said gruffly. "You pegged me as a shifter earlier, you might as well know what I am."

"A griffin shifter." Her eyes—didn't shine, exactly. The expression in them was more complicated than that. "Pine Valley is full of surprises. Dragons, hellhounds, a pegasus... and now a griffin shifter. When did you move here?"

"I didn't." To her silent question, he added, "I'm on vacation. A week's... decompression... and then back to work. I'm a detective."

"You're a detective? That sounds like a difficult job." And she was definitely looking uncomfortable now.

This whole hell of a situation just kept getting worse.

Hardwick snorted. "I'm better suited for it than most," he said. *Moment of truth.* "My griffin can tell when people are lying."

He watched her react, and the sudden flash of understanding mixed with terror and regret on her face made him feel almost regretful, himself. Then she pulled herself together so quickly he could almost taste her drawing more lies around herself, and he was on his guard again.

Her face closed over. The absence of any expression was the only hint he had that she was thinking like mad beneath the surface—but he was convinced she was.

*Who is this woman?*

# 7

# DELPHINE

"Oh… *good*," Delphine croaked. Hardwick's eyes twitched. "That does sound useful. For a detective."

*Fuuuuuuck*, she thought to herself.

He could tell when people were lying? Then he already knew that she'd lied to him. The question was: how much?

Was it a detailed thing? If she said something untrue, could he home in on the truth based on that, or would he just know that that specific thing was a lie? Could she—

She bit down on the inside of her cheek. Could she be honest with herself about what she was planning to do here?

Could she lie to the man she thought was her soulmate?

Could she not?

She was taking too long. The pause was becoming suspicious. She nestled in among her blankets and wrapped her hands around her coffee mug gratefully. The warmth inside the cabin and the woolen blankets had driven most of the chill from her limbs, but it was winter. No matter how warm you already were, a hot drink was always welcome.

She took a sip of the coffee and almost choked.

Well. A hot drink was *almost* always welcome. Had he used coffee for this, or gravel?

"I'm here on vacation, too," she said. "Along with what feels like most of my family, though I'm sure I'm forgetting a few second cousins who've managed to slip under the radar."

"And you're all winged lion shifters?"

The question was casual enough. As casual as her idiotic sip of coffee had been, and just as much of a mind-game. Delphine resisted the urge to narrow her eyes at him.

He *knew* she was lying. And he was—testing her? Teasing her?

She should have felt outraged—or really, terrified, given what the truth would do if it came out—but instead she felt an excited fizz down her spine.

Fine. If he wanted to play? She could play. She still felt off-balance, like she wasn't sure whether he was seriously interrogating her or just bantering, but this was... almost fun.

"For untold generations. Or told generations, if my Aunt Grizelda manages to corner you when she's in a genealogy mood."

Did that count as a lie? The bit about Aunt Grizelda was almost too true. Was avoiding the fact that *one* member of the current generation was not a winged lion shifter close enough to the truth?

His eye flickered again, but she couldn't tell whether that was because she'd hidden a lie in her answer, or he'd just swallowed another mouthful of coffee. Honestly, the stuff was dreadful. Which she reminded herself by taking another sip and choking it down before adding:

"The others are all visiting with the Heartwells today—do you know them?"

Hardwick shook his head.

"Dragon shifters. I met them last year. They live in a secluded valley a few miles out of town, where they can fly without being seen. I know a lot of my cousins were looking forward to stretching their wings after being cooped up in a plane for ten hours. My brothers, too. I just hope they actually waited until they got up there before shifting. I've had enough experience getting winged shifters un-stuck from inside cars to last a lifetime."

All true. All perfectly inane, perfectly true small talk.

And she knew what he was about to ask next. She could see it in his eyes. So, she got in first.

"I would have l-loved to go flying, too. But my grandfather wanted some groceries picked up from this specialist store down the mountain, so I was happy to offer to run the errand."

Hardwick winced. Delphine almost did, too. What a slip-up. Of course she wouldn't have loved to go flying. She would have had to ride on one of her relatives, and what better way to reveal that she couldn't shift?

It couldn't have been the other thing she said that was a lie. She *had* been happy to run around after Grandfather's port. More than happy. Overjoyed. Ecstatic. Relieved beyond belief.

That counted as happy, didn't it?

"Of course, by now the port's probably frozen and everyone's wondering where on Earth I am," she continued.

Hardwick raised one eyebrow. "Seems like a lot of trouble to go to for some booze," he remarked.

"Less trouble than Grandfather without his favorite tipple, trust me." She tipped her head back and smiled. "You're going to say something like 'Really? Less trouble than getting stuck in the snow and almost dying?' but honestly? If I haven't managed to deliver the goods, then being stuck out here in the snow is a net good. Potential concussion included."

"You don't have a concussion."

"Oh? Shall we test that? I don't have a concussion." She repeated his words, careful not to sound like she was asking a question, then raised one eyebrow at Hardwick. "Was that a lie?"

"If you do, you shouldn't be drinking that coffee." He leaned forward, staring deep into her eyes one after the other. "Your pupils look fine, and you remember what you were doing right before you hit your head—right?"

"Right."

*And shifters can shrug off a little thing like a concussion like it's nothing, anyway.* She waited for him to say it; it was the obvious next step in their game of I-can-tell-you-are-lying cat and mouse.

Instead, he frowned at her coffee mug. "No dizziness, nausea, loss of taste?"

"No."

His face cleared. "Good."

Delphine should have been relieved. A lack of concussion was generally considered to be a good thing. And Hardwick treating her potential concussion seriously was a good thing, too.

Instead, she felt irritated and off-balance.

The electric energy that had snapped between them as they traded questions and almost-lies had vanished. Had she imagined it entirely? Hardwick was being so… professional. As though she was just some random woman whose life he'd saved, and not the love of his life.

*What if I'm not?*

The thought hit her like a punch in the gut. She turned her jerk of surprise into a pretend shiver and nestled more deeply into the blankets.

What if she wasn't Hardwick's mate?

It was possible. After all, she wasn't a shifter. She wouldn't *know*-know like he would. How had her mother described meeting her father? The certainty, the feeling of everything else in the world losing focus… and her inner animal had told her that they were meant to be together.

She didn't have an inner animal to tell her anything. The certainty she'd felt when she first laid eyes on Hardwick was—well, not quite fading, but becoming wobblier the more time she spent in his presence. And of *course* the rest of the world had lost focus. She'd just almost *died*. Of *course* her brain would zero in on the person who saved her life.

And Hardwick…

He wasn't *acting* like a person who'd just been smacked around the back of the head with a whole quiver of Cupid's arrows. He was looking at her like she was exactly what, for all intents and purposes, she appeared to be: a young woman who'd gotten herself in trouble through her own stupidity, whom he'd had to interrupt his vacation to save, and who was less love's darling dream than… an irritation.

Her heart half-leaped, half-sank, with the result that it felt like it was ripping itself in two.

What a fool she was. This griffin shifter wasn't her mate; he was just the man who'd saved her life. And then her heart, in full damsel mode, had clung to him like he was Prince Charming. It wasn't a shifter thing. It was a fully human, fate-free thing.

She was relieved. Wasn't she? Of course she was.

"I do remember what I was doing before I fell in the snow," she said, her voice slightly shaky. And what was that about?

*Shaky with relief,* she told herself.

"I was about to get the car out of the ditch." There. Much steadier.

Across the room, Hardwick shifted uncomfortably, as though he had a sudden cramp.

"I wasn't thinking straight. Or—I thought I was at the time. I thought I could get myself out fine. I was going to put the chains on the car, which I thought was a fine idea at the time, except *how* I thought I was going to do that when the car was already arse-up in a ditch I don't know, and it doesn't matter anyway, because I couldn't even get back in the bloody car without knocking myself unconscious. And!"

Hardwick had opened his mouth, but he snapped it shut again.

"And did I even knock myself out? I hit my head, sure, but I don't think I'd be able to shout this much if I hit it hard enough to lose consciousness! Was it the cold? Because now that I think about it, I was out in the cold for far longer than anyone sensible would have been! And I took my gloves off, and I… I did so many stupid things!"

She was angry. Why was she angry? Because she almost died? Or because she'd decided that Hardwick couldn't be—

Her eyes locked on to him. He looked different, somehow, and it took her a moment to figure out why. The deep, stressed lines around his mouth and between his eyes were less deep. The tension that had seemed to crackle through his whole body every time he looked at her had eased.

Damn. All it took was her having one tiny breakdown, and suddenly her rescuer looked less like he wanted to throw up?

She pressed her palms against her face. "I thought I was thinking, but I wasn't. If you hadn't found me…"

"But I did. It's—" He sounded reluctant as he added, "it's best not to think about what might have happened if I had not."

"But *how* did you find me?" He was right, there was nothing to be gained from thinking about all the ways she could have died through her own stupid fault. But that wasn't going to stop her from digging into what *had* happened. If she was going to explain all this to her family, she'd need to get her story straight.

"I... heard you." Hardwick grimaced, as though he'd just sucked down another mouthful of coffee. But his cup was still in his hand, resting on his lap.

Delphine frowned. "You heard me? It's not like I was calling for help. And I'm sure I would have noticed if this cabin was anywhere near where I crashed. I might have lost it, but I wouldn't have missed a whole house with lights on and everything."

"You wouldn't have seen the cabin. We're about a mile away from your car—"

"A mile away? How did you hear me from so far away?"

Hardwick's jaw twitched. "I told you my griffin can sense lies."

Delphine flushed bright red. He'd found her because he sensed that she was *lying?* What had she said that was a lie when she was stuck out there by herself? She searched her memory, determined to find that he was mistaken. Okay, she lied to her family, but she didn't lie to *herself.*

Hardwick flinched.

She'd tried to boost her morale. Told herself that she would be okay. That wasn't a lie, was it? That she could handle things. Maybe in the technical, objective sense they'd been lies, but she hadn't meant them as such at the time. She'd thought they were the truth. Or that speaking them aloud could make them the truth.

And then she'd said—

Cold dripped down her spine, worse than the snowstorm Hardwick had saved her from.

She'd said *I am a real Belgrave, damn it.*

Was that what he'd sensed?

Oh, God. Oh God oh God oh God—

"Delphine." Strong hands caught hers. One of them moved to her shoulder, then her chin. He pushed her head up. "Breathe. You're safe now."

Safe wasn't the problem.

"On my count. In, two, three. Hold, two, three. Out, two, three…"

Slowly, with the help of Hardwick's breathing instruction, Delphine clawed herself back together.

*Don't think about it.* The realization she'd pulled herself out of was a black hole sucking at her attention and it took all of her strength to avoid it. She blinked hard and found herself staring into Hardwick's black eyes.

Her stomach tightened. Every point of connection between his body and hers suddenly flared with heat. His hand was wrapped securely around hers, the calluses pressing against her soft skin. His other hand under her chin, so intimate she worried he could feel her pulse thundering against his fingers. He'd moved to her so quickly that one of his legs was pressed up against hers and even though there were layers and layers of blanket between them, she was suddenly imagining what it would be like for him to slide his leg between hers, spreading her beneath him, hot and languid and longing.

"Uh," she muttered, breaking eye contact as heat flooded to her cheeks. "Sorry about that. I was... I... freaked out."

"It's understandable."

"It's *embarrassing*." As embarrassing as the way her heart was fluttering in her chest. Of all the people to get a crush on, she had to pick a shifter—someone whose heart was always going to be on hold for someone else?

She pulled her hand out of his. At the same time, he withdrew, as though he'd suddenly realized he was sitting too close to her.

"I'll get you something to eat," he said. "There's not much—I wasn't expecting company."

"I'll be out of your hair as soon as possible," she reassured him. "My phone was out of range. Is yours still dropping? Does the cabin have a landline?"

He shook his head. "Mine's barely on half a bar out here. And I get the feeling we're lucky the cabin has a generator. No phone, no internet."

"Not even for emergencies?"

"I think they expect the people who rent this place to either be self-sufficient or far enough up their own ass to think they are."

*And which are you?* The words were on the tip of her tongue, but she held them in. He shot her an amused look, like he'd guessed what she was about to ask.

"Neither of us will be flying anywhere until the blizzard runs its course, anyway." There was something careful in the way he said *neither of us.* Blast. She should have just told him the truth—

Except if they were stuck up here together for any length of time, and her family *did* come looking for her, then they'd meet him. No. Let him think she was a weirdo pretending to be a shifter. What did it matter to her?

Out loud, she said: "Blizzard? I know it was snowing earlier, but…"

She gathered one blanket around herself like a cloak and went to the nearest window. When she peered behind the curtain, the first thing she saw was a whole lotta nothing.

While she was waiting for her pathetic human eyes to adjust, she took advantage of the darkened window's mirror qualities to watch Hardwick in the kitchen. Which probably wasn't helping her eyes adjust to the darkness, but, she reasoned, she'd made plenty of mistakes already today. At least this one had some nice rewards.

Like the sight of Hardwick leaning over to grab something out of the freezer.

She bit back a sigh. The man was a tall, rangy creature straight out of a Western, and that was apparently completely her type. His shirt didn't strain at the seams like the guys her cousins drooled over, but the way he moved spoke of a controlled, contained strength that the usual recipients of Belgrave ogling didn't possess. Those guys tended to be more open about their muscles. But Hardwick…

Delphine turned her attention back to the world outside, where snow was gusting against the windows so hard, she was amazed she hadn't noticed it before. Then again, had she really been looking? Had she even really checked if her eyes needed to adjust before spying on her rescuer?

She closed her eyes. *You need to get a hold of yourself.*

"How long until it blows over?" she asked.

In the reflection, Hardwick shrugged. "Who can say?"

Delphine closed her eyes and rested her forehead against the window.

So, this was the situation. She was stuck in the middle of nowhere, without any way to tell her family where she was or why she was stuck, or of telling how long it would be until she could leave.

That was a lot of *withouts*. Despite everything, it was the *with* that worried her the most.

With Hardwick.

With a man who made her body react in ways it hadn't for anyone before.

And not only her body. Hardwick knew her secret, she was sure of it, but she wasn't panicking, or planning out ways to make this not a disaster, or trying to convince him that he was wrong and everything was just as she said it was. The idea of Hardwick knowing, of *anyone* knowing, she wasn't a shifter should have been devastating. The first crumbling of foundations that could send her whole life falling down.

Instead, it felt… good.

She straightened and shook herself.

It didn't matter how it felt. What mattered was getting through the next few days and coming up with a good story for her family. Not being able to fly during a blizzard—that was a good start.

And she wasn't Hardwick's mate.

That was good, too. It meant that as soon as the blizzard was over and she could go back into town, she could leave his discovery of the truth behind her.

It wouldn't matter that he knew her secret, because they weren't going to be a part of each other's lives.

# 8

## HARDWICK

Every breath was agony.

The frozen pizza had been the last thing Hardwick wanted to serve a woman like Delphine, but it was all he had that could be cooked quickly enough. Her head was drooping before she'd finished eating.

He'd given her the bed. What a mistake that had been. Now he was lying on the sofa where she had lain as she regained consciousness, where she'd sat to drink and eat. Her scent had caught on the cushions, the blanket... even the air.

And if that wasn't enough, his ears strained for every sound from the next room. The slight creak of the bed as she rolled over. Her soft, relaxed breaths, so much surer and steadier than her breathing had been when he pulled her from the—

The memory crashed over him. Her face, half-buried in the snow and so much paler than the healthy gold and warm flush that had spread across her face once she was awake. She hadn't moved at all; her limbs had hung limply when he picked her up. If it hadn't been for the way she kept muttering words under her breath, he might have thought he was too late.

Hardwick's griffin swiped at him. He bent his head, acknowledging its disgust.

Because of course it wasn't just her murmuring that had reassured him she was alive. It was the way the closer he got to her, the worse the pain got. A hammer against his skull, beating harder with each whispered word.

Almost everything she said hurt. When it didn't, his griffin was so suspicious for her next lie that it was hardly a respite; even if she set the hammer down, there was a strange, constant ache. He would have put it down to his griffin's end-of-year exhaustion, but there was something more to it than that.

He'd never met someone so sick with lies.

His griffin hissed and ground its beak. Hardwick groaned.

*I know, I know. How am I any better?*

He hadn't lied.

But he hadn't told the truth, either. Not the bit of it that mattered.

Somehow, in the midst of the ache in his head and his heart, he must have fallen asleep, because eventually he woke up.

Delphine was already up. Her footsteps were light, but sure—until he stirred. She spun around.

"Good morning." Her voice was low, with no trace of the surprise her feet had betrayed. "I thought I'd get breakfast on, since you cooked last night."

"Breakfast?" His mouth was moving ahead of his mind, echoing Delphine's words before he'd managed to put thought to them. He shook his head.

His brain was still lagging, but this time it was his eyes that snuck ahead.

Delphine was standing at the iron stove, her hair pulled back in a single thick, untidy braid and her cheeks flushed. Her arms were dusted with flour and there were white handprints on her front.

She followed his gaze down to the floury handprints and patted at them uselessly. "I didn't see an apron."

"I'm surprised you found flour."

Her eyebrows both rose. "In the pantry? I thought it must be yours. Perhaps the last person to stay here left it. Flour, baking powder, cheese, and butter. Just the basics, but…" She trailed off.

It took Hardwick a moment to realize he was expected to pick up the conversation. "You can blame me for the cheese. The rest must have been left over from a previous tenant, like you said."

He left unsaid that his idea of 'just the basics' was the contents of the frozen meal section at his local corner store.

"You're to blame for the cheese, huh? A man after my own h—"

She broke off suddenly. The color that flashed across her face now wasn't the lively warmth that had tugged at his memories again and again as he waited to fall asleep. It was a deep, strangled red.

"I—er—" Her eyes caught on his, like a fish to a lure.

He half-rose. Something inside him was rising to a crescendo, a wave about to break.

Then she looked away. "Cheese scones," she said, her shoulders rising. "Or—you probably call them biscuits. Cheese biscuits. These old coal-fired ovens can be tricky to get the hang of, but my grandmother has one quite like this. She always let me practice cooking on it."

Something skittered just beneath the surface of her words, close enough to a lie to scratch claws behind his eyes.

*My grandmother has one*—True.

*She always let me practice cooking on it*—Something there, an itch that his griffin couldn't let go.

*She always let me*—

That was it? The lie was that her grandmother *let* her use the oven? What was the alternative, that Delphine had barged in and taken over the kitchen?

Hardwick shook his head.

He washed up and changed his clothes, and by the time he ran out of excuses not to go back into the main room, the whole cabin was filling with the smell of baked dough and hot cheese.

Whatever strange urge was making him drag his feet couldn't compete with that.

Hardwick muttered his thanks for the meal as he sat down opposite her.

Delphine had set the table—something he wouldn't have thought possible, given the cabin's thin provisions. A stack of hot, butter-yellow biscuits steamed gently on a plate in the middle of the table. There was a stick of butter on another plate to one side, and two mugs of what smelled like the same deathly coffee he'd made the night before.

He didn't know where she'd found the butter. By the condensation dripping from the stick laid out on the kitchen table, and the way it fought the knife he tried to cut through it, he suspected it had been frozen. How long had she been up before he woke, to work this sort of magic?

"Oh, it's nothing," she murmured when he asked how she'd found it all. The lie scratched, though there was no sign of it on her face. "I like to get up early and make myself useful. Well, I always do, anyway."

Another lie. But—her final sentence was closer to the truth. Hardwick frowned. Had she forgotten he could sense untruths?

"How did you sleep?" he asked, tempting fate.

"Poorly." Her mouth quirked at his surprise. "I'm sorry. I know I should be a better guest, but there's no point lying, is there?"

"No."

"No." She echoed him, her voice making the word more musical than his had done.

He cleared his throat. "Were you too cold? I only arrived yesterday afternoon. I don't know if the heat gets through well enough to the other room."

"Mmm. No. I think my restless sleep had more to do with being in a strange bed, snowed in miles from anywhere, than it did room temperature."

Pain shot through Hardwick's forehead. He jerked one hand up to rub it, and when he lowered it again, Delphine was watching him. Her eyebrows were drawn together.

"You—" she began, and stopped herself. "You said last night that you're a detective?" she said after a brief hesitation. "That must be interesting, with your, um, particular skills."

"It's a living." Hardwick eased himself into the familiar conversation. It was the same one he had with other shifters who knew about his shifter type. Usually those conversations ended with the other person sloping off before the small talk got too close to the bone. "I have a gift. It's my duty to use it."

"Any good stories?"

He thought about the sting that had gone wrong and left Jackson with the scar from a bullet wound across his forehead. How a job that had been simple when he was a new recruit had turned into such a tangled mess.

But this was his *duty*. What was his gift for, except to help people?

Anyway, he had a story. Something from early in his career, featuring a lost kitten, two neighbor kids communicating with tin-can phones like something from the 1950s, and the sort of convoluted scheme that only a pair of eight-year-olds caught in their own lies would come up with. Bland and inoffensive. *Cute.*

"...and it turned out there were two kittens, after all, which explained the collar changing color. Every time their parents got suspicious and they handed off what they thought was the *only* kitten to what they thought was the other kid, one of the kittens got picked up by the old lady who was living downstairs."

"It's like that puzzle with the wolf, the sheep, and the cabbage," Delphine said. "What happened to the kittens afterwards?"

"I don't know." Hardwick searched his memory, but his griffin was sure that his automatic response had been the truth.

"Back to the pound, I suppose, if they weren't allowed in the apartments." Delphine's voice had an undertone of pessimism that made his attention jerk towards her.

"It's a happier ending than most," he said.

"Even with your gift?"

"People don't need my gift because they were already having a good day."

Delphine made a face and gestured with her butter knife. "Point. Sugar for your coffee?"

He shook his head and she spooned sugar into her own mug, which she then looked at as though it was going to jump up and bite her. Which wasn't far wrong. Even his griffin agreed with that.

Hardwick wanted to be confused about why she was asking about his powers when it was so obvious she knew he'd seen through her attempts to lie about who—*what*—she was. But he wasn't. Even though it made his heart ache and his griffin hide its head under its wing, he knew the main reason people gathered information like that was to find a way around it.

She was getting better. He had to give her that. His griffin was having to peck out her lies, untangle them from words that were mostly truth. But everything she said was still hazed around with a fog of deceit. It was as though her whole being was a lie.

Despite his better judgment, he found himself wanting to know more.

The 'scones' were good.

*Really* good.

And not just because they were delicious. Hardwick tried to remember the last time anyone had cooked for him. Picking up a coffee from the station cafeteria didn't count.

Hell, when was the last time he'd cooked for himself?

Most days, by the end of his shift, he was too exhausted and in too much pain to do more than order takeout. Even when he was stocking up for this trip, he'd limited himself to readymade frozen meals and a few basics. It was some sort of miracle that Delphine had found enough ingredients to do any baking at all.

No. He gazed across the table. The miracle was that she'd *wanted* to cook for him.

She caught his stare and looked up. Her cheeks went pink. Hell. What was he doing? He had to tell her the truth. Had to—

"I'd really like to try and get back to Pine Valley today," Delphine said.

Pain shot through his forehead. Hardwick dropped his knife with a clatter. He was half-aware of Delphine getting up from the table and he waved her away, his gesture jerky as he tried to breathe through his griffin's reaction.

His griffin cowered inside him, puffing itself up to make it look bigger. Hardwick clutched his hand to his forehead. Calm down, he told himself, or his griffin, or both. Breathe through it. It'll fade soon.

Slowly, reluctantly, his griffin's feathery ruff deflated. It settled itself back on its haunches, tail flicking.

And the pain faded.

Hardwick sighed. "Sorry, bud," he whispered, rubbing his forehead.

"What was that?"

Delphine looked like she was sitting down by sheer force of will alone. Her hands were braced on the edge of the table. Her eyes bored into his. If she'd been a shifter, her inner animal would have been blazing out through her gaze, demanding the same answer.

But she was human, and the blazing was all her.

"Migraine," Hardwick gritted out. "They've been getting bad lately. Give it a minute, it'll pass."

Until the next time she casually lied to him.

Even that circle-round-the-truth made his griffin pace warily. Hardwick muttered something that he deserved a rap across the knuckles for and forced the pained grimace off his face.

"Thank you for breakfast," he said, meeting Delphine's blazing glare with a mild expression of his own. "It's delicious. Really. Can't remember the last time I had anything this good."

Her eyes widened. Some of the fire in them faded—and then they narrowed sharply. "You're serious. Because you don't lie."

"Right."

"They're *scones*." She looked outraged. "They take no effort! All sorts of food are better than them! Haven't you been looking after yourself?"

Her mouth dropped open as though hadn't meant to say that last bit. Or any of it, Hardwick mused.

She recovered quickly. "Not that it's any of my business," she added, mildly, and a serrated knife-edge ran around the base of his skull.

Lie.

She *did* think it was her business.

Hardwick's mouth was suddenly dry. He sipped his coffee. Didn't help.

What if she knew?

Or if she didn't know, what if she could guess? The connection between them. The way he couldn't stop himself from turning towards her, his constant awareness of her every mood, the changing expressions on her face and the hidden thoughts and emotions she tried not to let show.

He didn't know how humans experienced the mate bond. They didn't have an inner creature to tell it to them straight. But they couldn't be completely unaffected, could they?

Delphine couldn't be. The emotion blazing from her eyes wasn't anything that could be explained by her just seeing him as some random asshole who'd saved her life. When he doubled over, she hadn't backed away, like any sensible person would when the stranger they were sharing a cabin with started behaving strangely.

She wasn't just concerned, she was *mad*.

He sorted through what he knew. They both knew where things stood with his abilities—didn't they? He could tell when she was telling the truth. She knew he could tell when she was telling the truth. Neither of them had said anything about any connection between them.

*She* hadn't said anything.

Why not?

"None of your business," he repeated, his voice a gravelly rasp. "You sure about that?"

Her eyes narrowed further. Excitement fluttered in his stomach, a bright spark that drove the last of the pain in his head away. This wasn't lying. This was a game. Wasn't it?

Delphine held his gaze for a minute that seemed to stretch on forever. The air between them almost sang with tension.

Then she looked away.

"There are only a few things in my life I'm sure of," she said, her eyes still averted. "One of them is that I feel like I should get back to my family as soon as I can. The snow's stopped. If you can take me back to my car…"

Hardwick's stomach dropped. "Of course."

No point telling himself that what he was feeling wasn't disappointment. Or confusion. The energy that had sparked between them—she must have felt it. And if she was from a shifter family, she must know what it meant.

Which meant she was deliberately avoiding it. Their connection. *Him.*

The sinking in his stomach turned into a pit. His appetite disappeared. He stood up.

"We'd better get moving before the weather turns again," he said. "Let me know when you're ready."

# 9

## DELPHINE

Delphine tidied herself up in the tiny bathroom and wondered what the hell she was doing.

Hardwick wasn't her mate. That was obvious, wasn't it? He wasn't her mate, and he wasn't interested in her hanging around, so why had it been so difficult to tell him she wanted to go back to her car?

It wasn't even a lie. At least, she thought it wasn't. Ugh, she hated having to second-guess everything she was saying like this.

At least life with her family was simple. She knew exactly what each of them expected of her, and fulfilling those expectations was the easiest thing in the world.

Even if they didn't expect a lot from her.

She hissed in a breath. The thought had bubbled up before she could stop it. She tried to push it away, but it just loomed larger.

Her family *didn't* expect a lot from her.

How could they?

She'd spent most of her life putting herself in a very specific box. She wasn't fun to be around, like her brothers, or wickedly opinionated, like her cousin Pebbles, or on track to discover the next big cancer breakthrough like everyone said Brutus was going to do. She was just… there. Or *not* there, most of the time. In the background, being helpful and keeping out of the way.

Never looking anyone in the eye, in case they noticed there was no winged lion looking back at them. Never replying to any telepathic conversation. She'd accepted years ago that that meant her relatives would think she was either a snob or stupid, and she'd been fine with it. Hadn't she?

If she told Hardwick she was fine with it, would he look at her like she'd just admitted to kicking puppies?

She smoothed down her sweatshirt. Her hands were shaking.

It was a good thing she was going back to town, if just one night around Hardwick was messing her up like this.

*If I said that to Hardwick, would he—*

She shook her head firmly. She had to stop thinking like that.

And *start* thinking about what she would tell her family when she got back to the hotel.

If they were at the hotel. She ran over the holiday schedule in her mind. Yesterday, her grandfather had planned to visit the Heartwells so the younger lions could go flying out of sight of the town and the older ones could bask in the various ways they decided they were superior to the dragon shifters.

She didn't need to be there to know that was the plan. The only reason her grandparents ever thought other varieties of shifters were worth talking to was to cement their position as the top of the heap. Winged lions with pedigrees going back thousands of year were just *better* than everyone else, don't you know?

At least she wouldn't have to pretend to already know what had happened there. So far as everyone else was concerned, she'd been out of range of even the loudest telepathic shrieks. Which meant there was an opportunity for conversation. Maybe Aunt Grizelda would like to give her a blow-by-blow of the visit, and that could keep her out of having to do... whatever was on the cards for today.

Dogsledding? Ice-skating?

She couldn't remember.

Delphine stared at herself in the mirror, horrified. She couldn't remember? She *always* remembered. Remembering was how she got everything done. Not even the most complicated scheduling app could keep up with Mr. Petrakis's wayward planning, and she'd developed those skills through long years with her family. If she couldn't remember where they were meant to be, how could she arrange her own life to be in the perfect place to avoid anyone confronting her?

She leaned over the battered tin sink, breathing heavily.

*I should stay here.*

The thought was tempting. Too tempting. And ridiculous. What was she thinking? How could spending more time in this run-down, practically falling-down shack, with a man who looked sick every time she spoke to him, be preferable to spending Christmas with her own family? Yes, she'd been happy enough to spend a night away from them by herself, but this was... was...

She pushed herself away from the sink and walked swiftly back into the main room.

Where Hardwick was waiting for her.

"You'll want this," he said gruffly, holding out a coat. It was bigger and thicker than Delphine's, designed entirely for warmth instead of partially for warmth and partially for fashion. And chosen, she had to admit, because to choose a winter coat built *only* for warmth would be to admit that she had a frail human body that needed extra insulation.

Unless, apparently, you were Hardwick, whose clothing choices were more sensible than all the Belgraves combined.

"Thank you." She shrugged the jacket on. It swamped her shoulders and reached down to her knees. Warmth surrounded her, and she remembered why the thought of staying here with Hardwick was more than just ridiculous.

It was dangerous.

Because the longer she spent with Hardwick, even with his grumpy face and the obvious resentment with which he treated her presence, the more she was tempted to tell him the truth. About her, and her family, and everything she'd done to keep a wall of lies between them.

She didn't understand it. She *couldn't* understand it. It made no sense. But in between the awkwardness and the feeling of rubbing up his fur the wrong way and, oh, God, the lying awake the night before unable to stop thinking about the fact that he was right there in the next room, crammed onto the sofa she'd been sitting on only a few hours before, possibly undressed or even partially undressed…

…Quite apart from any of that, she'd enjoyed talking to him. Once she figured out that *he'd* figured out that she wasn't actually a shifter, talking to him had—eventually—been relaxing in a way she'd forgotten conversation could be. She'd wanted to know about his work, and his powers, and he'd told her, without her having to hedge her side of the conversation with rubbish about how *her* inner animal did such-and-such, or how her job was perfect for a winged lioness, because it combined the Belgraves' essential traits of sucking up to other mythical shifters while pretending they were better than them, or something.

And he hadn't pushed her to talk about herself. He'd known she was lying about being a shifter, and he'd just… let her lie.

Which on top of everything else, was a terrible reason for her to want to tell him everything. Was she really so self-centered that some guy not wanting to know her innermost secrets made her determined to serve them up to him?

She couldn't, anyway. This wasn't about her. It was about the same thing Belgraves were always about.

Family.

# 10

# HARDWICK

"**I** take it I'll be flying us down."

Hardwick had thought that went without saying, but the shock on Delphine's face—quickly hidden—told him that she'd forgotten that particular detail.

A sudden surge of frustration gripped him. How could she forget something so simple? Almost everything she said was a lie. What sort of fraud made a slip like that?

*One who crashed her car and almost died, and spent the night dealing with your ugly face treating her like she was on the other side of the interview table?*

Sometimes he wondered if his griffin would be as hard on him as he was himself, if it could talk.

"Oh... yes." Delphine bit her lower lip and Hardwick had to look away.

He wanted to say so much more but forced himself to go outside. He'd cleared a path through the newly fallen snow while she was getting ready. Snow was heaped in against the sides of the cabin, but the flat space out the front wasn't too deeply blanketed in the stuff. The carport was a pure white cube. His own truck was somewhere inside it.

None of which boded well for the state of Delphine's rental.

They could deal with that when they got to it.

Delphine followed him out, wrapped up in his winter coat and gloves over her own jacket. Her own scarf and hat looked incongruous next to his clothing; his stuff was heavy and dark, thick wool half-felted with age and wear, while hers were dainty, pale blue with matching snowflake patterns.

She pushed her hands deep into his pockets and he hoped like hell he hadn't left an old handkerchief or worse in there.

Hardwick rolled his shoulders back. "How much experience do you have flying?"

It wasn't meant as a challenge. Delphine clearly took it as one, anyway. She gave him a long, hard sideways look.

"…None being flown around by someone else," she said carefully, and it was the truth.

"Can't say I have much experience flying anyone else around, myself."

"How did you get me up here yesterday?"

"Grabbed you in my claws."

She went slightly pale. "Let's try something else," she suggested. "Sometimes when my family's all together, we—uh, my brothers and cousins—will shift mid-air and practice landing on each other's backs. To mess up each other's flying. And they take the younger kids for rides, sometimes…"

"But not you?"

Her expression jerked strangely. "We didn't spend a lot of time with the family when I was big enough that my parents would have let me, and not yet the age where I… where… most Belgraves start being able to shift for themselves." Her shoulders hunched.

That's a story with a lot missing, Hardwick thought.

But it was more of a story than he'd expected. And more truth than he'd expected, too.

"We can try that," he said out loud. "You on my shoulders?"

Delphine nodded, but didn't make any move. He sighed. "I know some shifters don't care about this sort of thing, but I'd prefer it if you turned around."

"Oh!" Delphine spun around. "I'm sorry, I thought—"

"What?" Hardwick pulled off his shirt. The air was dry and still, but even with that and his natural shifter hardiness, he only had a few minutes before the cold started to get to him. "Belgraves are all nudists, or something?"

It wouldn't be unusual. Plenty of shifters had lower boundaries around nudity than humans did.

Hardwick was the same, when the person he was being ass naked in front of wasn't his mate.

"Belgraves have jumped on the discovery that you *can* shift and take your clothes with you, actually." Her voice sparkled with amusement.

"You're shitting me."

"No, it's definitely a thing. They like to compete over how many expensive accessories they can bring with them without dissolving into a pile of sparks. One of my brothers has destroyed three phones in the last year messing it up."

"You'll have to tell me more about it—" Hardwick stopped himself. "Never mind."

Because after he dropped her off, there weren't going to be any opportunities for either of them to tell the other anything.

He checked to make sure she was still looking away, got ready to shuck off his pants and boots, and concentrated on his griffin. Just as he was about to shift, Delphine held up a hand.

"Wait!"

He cursed silently, held onto his pants, and waited.

Delphine didn't turn around. "I won't... be able to communicate with you when you're in your griffin form," she admitted.

"You can still talk to me. I'm the one who'll have trouble making myself heard."

The damned connection. It pricked at him, urging him to close the distance between them. He couldn't let himself do that physically.

But that wasn't the only option. She'd told him something of herself that she might not have intended, if she didn't know he'd be able to tell she was lying. He could return the gesture.

"Talking isn't the only way to communicate," he said. "My griffin doesn't talk at all, and we get on fine."

"It doesn't talk at *all*?" Delphine's eyebrows disappeared under her woolly hat. "I didn't know that was possible."

Hardwick shrugged. "Some people don't, so why not our animals? And like I said, we don't need words to get the message across. It uses sign language, I guess."

She spun around. "Does that mean you can *see*—"

He could sure as hell see the effort it took her to cut herself off. And the shame that tightened her face, pushing away the sudden, bright interest that had lit her up from the inside.

His jaw hardened. She never got to ask questions like this, did she? If she spent all her time pretending she already was a shifter and therefore knew all about it.

"Go on," he urged her gently.

She looked guilty. She actually glanced around the clearing, as though she was worried someone was listening in. "You can see your griffin, even when you're in human form?"

"Better than I can when I'm in griffin form. We don't exactly spend a lot of time sitting in front of a mirror." He watched her carefully. "If I close my eyes, I can bring it up. Like revisiting a memory, or a picture."

"And it communicates to you through sign language?"

"Body language would be more accurate. Movements, gestures."

*Or it just stares at me like I'm the world's biggest asshole.* Like it was doing then. He huffed out a breath. *All right, buddy. You want to be the one to tell her we're meant to be together, but every minute in her presence leaves me this much closer to a weeklong migraine?*

It shuffled its wings in unhappy acknowledgement.

"That's—" Delphine shook her head slowly. Some of the light was back in her eyes, now. Not all. "That makes sense. It's harder to lie with body language than with words."

Hardwick's jaw tightened again. That wasn't the message he'd meant her to get! He sighed, rubbing the side of his jaw where the muscles were starting to jump. "Let's just get moving."

"Promise if you need to say something to me while we're in the air, you'll wait to land before you try to tell me anything that involves barrel rolls or loop-the-loops?"

Hardwick let out a surprised bark of laughter. "I'll do my best."

His head was spinning as he tried to concentrate on shifting. Every time he thought he could put Delphine in a box—a box labelled 'liar' or 'too much trouble'—she said something that went straight to his heart. Or his funny bone, which was even more impressive. He hadn't thought he had one of those left.

And that second box didn't fit, anyway. He was the one who was too much trouble.

Delphine turned away again, and he focused on his griffin. Shifting was easier and harder than it had been the night before, when he and his griffin had both been frantic with worry for Delphine. Easier, because although he was used to managing his own fear response in difficult situations, he didn't have any experience with his griffin being in those situations. Harder, because without the urgency of saving Delphine's life, calling his griffin out was like trying to get a rusty engine to fire.

After a few moments, though, he began to transform. Lights danced in his eyes and he closed them, letting the shift take over as he cast off the rest of his clothing. There was a feeling like a cool wind blowing over his whole body and he dropped to all fours.

His griffin flexed its back, stretching out knots that his human body hadn't acknowledged. He scooped up his discarded clothing in one foreclaw and tossed it over to the cabin door. He—

Shit.

He was going to need those clothes for the other end of this little trip.

He paced over to the door and hooked his trousers on one claw. While he was still trying to decide on the least embarrassing and most efficient way to act out 'could you carry my clothes for me while I fly you to your car,' Delphine turned to face him.

Her eyes went wide.

Hardwick's griffin was nothing special. He knew that. His parents had both been griffin shifters; his mom's feathers were a brilliant, shimmering mahogany merging into silver-dusted hindquarters, and his father had gleaming black feathers with hints of gold at his chest and around his eyes.

Hardwick was grey. Shabby grey, from beak to tail.

"Gosh," Delphine breathed. "You're—I mean—I've never seen a griffin before." Her eyebrows drew together, and she pursed her lips, as though she was thinking over something quickly. "Which I already told you, and it *is* the truth. I thought you'd be more like a winged lion, but you're—"

He didn't want to hear what he was. His griffin flicked its tail, indicating its desire to get moving and leave this conversation behind. To his surprise, Delphine caught on at once.

She walked closer to him, her footsteps slow and careful in the snow. He tried not to shuffle his feet as her eyes coasted from his huge, grey-feathered eagle's head to his hindquarters the color of a lion who'd rolled around in a fireplace. "Behind your shoulders. Okay. Would you mind kneeling down?"

Standing, with his neck stooped, his eyes were almost level with Delphine's. He crouched down, snow crunching beneath claws and heavy paws as she moved towards him.

"Nothing to worry about. Just like getting on a horse," she muttered to herself, and his griffin hissed. Delphine jerked back. "Sorry! Sorry, I—wasn't thinking. I'll be more careful."

He was the one who needed to be careful. It was so much harder to disguise his griffin's reactions in this form. And although she knew he could tell when people were lying, he'd kept quiet about the pain it caused him. He didn't want her to know that the reason he was all the way out here in the mountains was that he was hiding.

Delphine put a gentle hand out to rest against his side. Her touch was muffled by the thick gloves she was wearing, but it was still touch. Deliberate touch.

He curled his talons more securely around his trousers. He would need to get dressed *fast* once he shifted back into human form.

"I'm going to use your fore-leg as a step," she warned him, then swung herself up. She overshot, and Hardwick moved beneath her to keep her balanced until she could steady herself. "Oof! I think I've got it now. Thank you."

She put one hand on each shoulder, gripping the bases of his wings where they sprouted from his back. Hardwick held still.

"No mane," she murmured. "I didn't think of that. I don't want to pull any of your feathers out."

Hardwick tried to shrug without dislodging her. She shifted her weight slightly, and the strange feeling of having someone on his griffin's back became, if no less strange, at least less precarious feeling.

"Okay." Her voice was more confident now. "Try standing up?"

Hardwick got to his feet. Slowly. Delphine's breathing shallowed nervously, but she didn't overbalance.

He looked back at her over his shoulder. She wasn't pale or showing any other tell-tale signs of fear. In fact, she looked cautiously excited.

He wondered if she would say as much. Ironic, really, that he was the one having to read her body language and not just the other way around.

His griffin tipped its head to one side. It wanted to get into the air; it wanted, Hardwick realized with a lurch, to show off.

"Is that you asking if I'm ready to take off?" Delphine looked over his head for a moment, past the ring of snow-covered trees around the edge of the clearing, to the cloud-thick sky. "Yes. I'm ready."

*All right*, he told it. *Easy, though.*

His griffin stretched out its wings. From above, it must have looked like someone had spread gravel in front of the cabin. He beat the air once, twice, testing it for lift and the small eddies of breezes that sifted through the trees, then on the third stroke leapt into the air.

The icy air wasn't the best for flying. It was even worse for flying from ground level, with a woman clinging to his back. He should have launched himself from the cabin roof—if he'd thought it would hold his weight.

Too late now. He beat his wings against the frigid air, fighting to gain enough height that he could simply glide the rest of the way to where Delphine had crashed her car.

Delphine's knees dug into his sides. And her elbows. Her hands twisted in the feathers just above his shoulders. Could sheer terror break a mate bond? He was sure he was about to find out.

Finally, he was far enough above the canopy that he could stop flapping and stretch his wings out. He made sure he was flying steady, then snuck a look at Delphine over his shoulder.

She was smiling as though her heart was about to burst with joy.

A ripple of warmth went through him. She caught his eye and her smile changed. The first smile had been open, unintentional, a straight transfer of feelings to expression.

This smile was for him. And this new smile wasn't hiding those feelings or translating them into something she thought he would prefer. It was inviting him to join in her happiness, her energy, the sheer joy radiating through her.

He didn't want the flight to end.

But soon enough, it did.

# II

# DELPHINE

T he mood changed as soon as Hardwick landed. No, that wasn't fair. There was no universal *mood* that changed. It was her. Her mood. Her workaday self, wrapping back around her true self like an old, itchy coat.

She wished the flight could have lasted longer. That she could have caught it and frozen it in place, like a scene in a snow globe, and never had to move on to deal with whatever was coming next.

Especially when what came next was this.

She frowned as she slipped down from Hardwick's back into knee-deep snow. The road looked nothing like what she remembered from the previous night. But it had been night, after all. The whole world had seemed ghostly and strange.

A memory from the night before rose up in her mind. Sitting in the car with the engine and all the lights off, and the darkness all around. No one watching. No expectations.

"Is this the right place?" she asked to distract herself from the unsettling sensation in her stomach. "Where's the car?"

Hardwick blinked at her. She could imagine the look that would have been on his face if he was in human form, and she didn't need fifteen years of decoding her relatives' moods when they were in animal form to translate the stiff-legged way he stalked to the side of the road. One swipe of his claws, then another, and the front bumper of her rental car appeared.

He shook snow off his legs and moved back. Delphine gaped.

She'd known it had been snowing, of course, but...

There was a good foot-and-a-half of snow above the car. Above the car's front bumper. More, over the rest of the car where it had fallen deeper into the ditch.

More, over the hole she must have made for herself, falling backwards into it. Much more.

Delphine swallowed.

She'd forgotten. Or let herself forget. She'd let Hardwick's lie-detecting powers, and what that meant, distract her. She'd twisted herself in circles trying to reason her way around the strange feelings that gripped her chest whenever she looked at Hardwick, or thought about him, or thought about him looking at her. And this part of yesterday's adventure had faded into the background.

If Hardwick hadn't gotten here when he did—

"Can you get it back on the road?" she blurted out.

The griffin gave her a sidelong glance that looked so much like his human expression that she had to bite her tongue to stop a burst of nervous laughter. Then he shrugged and moved closer to the snow-bound car.

He inspected the car, and she inspected him.

When he'd said he was a griffin shifter, she'd expected something like her winged lion relatives: a stocky, powerful lion body, with wings, and a bit of eagle. Hardwick's griffin form was nothing like that. The front half of his body, the eagle part, was streamlined and sharp. The lion part was lean and graceful. He looked like a creature made to glide through the air, not smash through it like winged lion shifters did. His feathers and fur melded seamlessly into one another, soft-looking grey that made her think of stones washed smooth by water, or the ash in a fireplace after a long, romantic evening.

Not romantic. A long something-else evening. Oh … good.

Hardwick jerked his head at her. She took his meaning and kicked her way through the snow until she was out of the way. She was beginning to wish she'd brought thicker trousers—or waterproof ones.

When her boss did venture to colder regions for his work, it was to places that were more decoratively snowy than deeply snowy. Last Christmas had been an exception, but she'd barely ventured beyond the town then.

Had Hardwick been here last year, as well?

What if he had been? What if they had met, with only her mother and brothers to worry about, and not her whole extended family? Would she have been more willing to entertain the thought that her sudden attraction to him was more than just a crush?

What if it was more?

Her first instinct was to grab the thought and hide it away. She forced herself to let it go and it rolled over her like a cool breeze.

What if what she felt for Hardwick was more than she'd let herself believe?

She'd lain in bed the night before, aggravatingly awake, her ears straining for any sound from the next room. She'd pressed her face into the pillow, searching for any sign of his scent—she didn't even know what he smelled like! They had barely touched. Just that moment on the sofa, when he'd gently checked the bruise on the back of her head.

Except he must have touched her before that. Carried her into the cabin, wrapped her in blankets. His hands around her back and legs, steadying her head as he laid her down, tucking the woolen blankets around her body.

Delphine gasped as heat surged through her. She could almost feel the ghostly pressure of Hardwick's hands on her. She was making it up, of course. She couldn't remember anything before she woke up on the sofa and by that time Hardwick had fled to the other side of the room.

But he'd been close to her. He'd touched her. Which meant he would *know*, surely, if they were mates.

She closed her eyes tight. *Why do I keep going back to this? Haven't I already decided it's nonsense?*

If she was Hardwick's mate, he would have said something.

Unless…

She went very still.

Unless he had a reason not to.

A reason like his mate being a woman who'd built her life around lying to the people who should love her the most. A woman who'd lied to *him*, first deliberately and then by omission.

The cold that stuck chill fingers down her back now had nothing to do with the weather. It crept inside her, stiffening her lungs, making her stomach clench.

And met a sudden, hot anger.

She wasn't the only one who'd been lying by *omission*.

With a screech of metal and snow grinding on snow and rock, Hardwick hauled the car up out of the ditch. He paused a moment, sides heaving with effort, then shoved it again, pushing it fully onto the flat. Snow cascaded off his wings as he settled them across his back and he turned to Delphine, dark eyes glittering.

This was it, she thought, as ice and fire met inside her to create something churning and awful. We're done. I've gotten everything I want: back to the car, and soon I'll be back with my family, and out of his hair. Everything is going to plan.

She searched inside herself for upbeat, professionally grateful and one hundred percent not on the edge of regretting all of her life choices and found an appropriate smile.

Hardwick looked uncomfortable. He glanced from the car, to Delphine, to the road behind her, and then let out a sigh that made his wings rustle. He moved behind the car and the air around him began to shimmer.

Delphine turned her back. It wasn't polite to watch people shift, she told herself, but it wasn't just that. Plenty of shifters were practically exhibitionists. But Hardwick had been shy about the no-clothes issue, so it would be especially wrong not to give him some privacy.

That wasn't it, either. The truth wormed into her mind. She turned away, because despite everything she told herself some hopeful part of her heart still believed he was her mate. But that couldn't be real. A decision she'd made over a decade ago, a decision she'd shaped her life around, meant that even if that was real, it couldn't happen.

And if it wasn't going to happen then she was *not* going to try to steal a glimpse of him.

"Delphine—"

She swallowed down a sudden lump in her throat and turned around. "You actually did it! Thank you so much. I am sorry to have taken so much of your time, but—"

"You don't seriously think you're going anywhere in that?"

Hardwick had been standing behind the car, but now he stalked around it. Her pulse spiked until he rounded the car and she saw he'd pulled on his trousers. He must have carried them with him.

What about the rest of his clothes?

"What are you talking about?" she asked, trying her best to ignore all the bits of Hardwick's body not covered by his trousers, but also not to stare at his trousers. "You got the car out—"

"Car's not the problem. The road is." He gestured behind her, and she tore her eyes away from not-his-chest and not-his-trousers.

He was right. The road, like the patch of flat ground she was standing on, like everything else she could see, was two feet deep in snow.

Her stomach dropped. "You'd better drop me back in town then."

"That's an hour's flight, at least." He added, reluctance in every angle of his body: "I don't know if you saw over the ridge while we were flying, but more snow's on its way. Looks heavier. It's going to get colder. I don't want to risk you losing your grip and falling off me or ending up flying blind in a blizzard with no shelter."

He was right. She had seen the snow, and realized, like him, that the calm surrounding the rustic cabin had been a lucky chance.

But him being right didn't make this any easier.

As she thought that, the first flakes of snow began to whisk through the air.

"Well I can't stay here!"

"No." His dark eyes caught hers, even through the flurrying snowflakes. "We'll have to go back to the cabin."

Before she could decide how she was going to answer that, let alone how she actually felt about it, he dug around in his trouser pocket and pulled something out.

"Good news is I've got signal. If you make it quick, you can call your folks, leave a message for them—"

"No!"

She didn't need to think. Possibly she should have. Yes, it would have been a good idea to stop for even half a second and think before shouting out that she didn't want to let her family know that she was alive and not dead in a ditch somewhere. Here. Dead in a ditch right here.

Her tongue stumbled over her next words. "I mean—that is—they don't know—"

Hardwick's eyes widened and she slammed her hands over her mouth before she told him everything.

Shit. She couldn't lie. He'd know at once. And he might have been willing to give her some leeway so far, but even the most incurious person in the world would wonder why she didn't want to tell her family where she was.

She had to tell him the truth.

Spine rigid, she thought of her grandparents, aunts and uncles and cousins, and twisted her tongue around the words: "They'll be happier if I don't get in touch."

Hardwick blinked at her. She couldn't read the expression on his face.

"You're telling the truth." He sounded dismayed.

"I thought it was about time I started." *She* sounded snappish.

"Do you want to talk about it?"

Delphine pulled her coat closer around herself. No, not her coat. Hardwick's coat.

He'd been so kind to her. Even if he was her mate, he deserved better.

But as for what she wanted…

"No." She looked him in the eye. "No. I really don't."

# 12

# HARDWICK

The flight back up to the cabin seemed faster than the flight down.

Probably because he wanted it to end even less than he had the first one.

His head was still aching when he shifted back into human form. That last lie had left him reeling in more ways than one. And the truth—

The truth had hurt even more. Not his head. His heart.

He just didn't understand her. But, God, he wanted to. The longer he spent in her company, the more he realized that his first suspicions that Delphine was running some sort of scam had been wrong.

This wasn't a woman who was gleefully pulling one over her shifter family. Delphine was scared.

And he was an asshole.

What was he meant to do?

He'd always thought that if he was lucky enough to find his mate, it would be easy. Like with his parents. They were both griffin shifters. Neither of them had lie-sensing powers as powerful as his—they had told him they got a feeling when someone lied around them, like something wasn't right, but it had never hurt. But they had both been honest enough people that the whole falling-in-love process was almost hilariously simple. They met and realized they were each other's mates; they got a marriage license and had a court wedding within the week. Not the most romantic of stories, but it was Hardwick's baseline for how these things were meant to work.

It wasn't meant to hurt.

And there was no way of avoiding hurt now. Hiding something like this from your mate was unforgivable. If Delphine's family were as traditional as she made them sound, then she would know what an insult it was to pretend someone wasn't your soulmate. He couldn't excuse himself for what he'd done. Maybe if she had left, if the road had somehow been miraculously clear enough and her car un-frozen enough that their initial plan had worked, he could have pulled off a romantic last-minute change of heart and chased after her.

Instead, they were both lurking around the cabin, trying to put as much distance between themselves and the other as possible.

Hardwick had exiled himself to the bedroom. He sat down on the bed, head in hands, and tried to think past the pain beating through his skull.

The bed was a mistake. Just like sleeping on the sofa the night before had been a mistake. Delphine had been in here, and her scent was on everything. The sheets, the pillow, the *air.*

And now—shit. She was back on the sofa right now. Which meant that tonight, when he tried to sleep—

He groaned and buried his face in the pillow. The pillow that smelled like Delphine. The woman who was meant to be his mate but who he could barely look at without his head hurting.

He stuck it out in the bedroom for another few hours. Every minute that ground by, he was acutely aware of Delphine in the next room. The sofa creaked slightly as she moved around; water hissed as she filled a glass.

He stared at his watch. Lunch time. No more excuses. Not if he wanted to seem like a halfway decent host, and not the surly prick that he'd probably come off as so far. Damn it.

Delphine looked up as he stood in the door. He had a strange impulse to knock on the doorframe. He cleared his throat. "Are you hungry?"

Her eyes fell to his mouth and her own lips parted, just briefly. He couldn't look away.

"Um—" Delphine swallowed.

"I'll make lunch," he said quickly.

Shit.

He'd told himself she was in shock. In shock, from almost dying, and then embarrassed, from being stuck here with him. But even non-shifters could feel something of the mate bond, couldn't they?

And her family were shifters. She must know what was going on. Which meant she knew he knew and that he wasn't doing anything about it, and now he knew she knew and... his head hurt.

And all he had to serve for lunch were frozen meals. He'd planned for this trip thinking he'd only be feeding himself. Not feeding his mate. Not that he was trying to seduce her.

Well, freezer-burned enchiladas were the perfect not-seducing food.

The meal took an excruciating hour to cook. Hardwick couldn't find an excuse to hide in the bedroom while they were in the oven—and it would have been hiding.

He just couldn't find an excuse to do anything else, either.

He stood like a lump by the oven, close to wishing he could hurl himself into it.

Delphine was not reading a book. By the time the enchiladas were ready he was pretty sure she was on the same page she'd been on when he started, and that page was page one. She wasn't looking at him, either. Her eyes were fixed on the page like she was trying to burn through it.

He looked at her. He couldn't help it.

There were dark shadows under her eyes that hadn't been there the night before. She'd said she slept badly, didn't she? Had she lain there in the bed, thinking about him as he thought about her? What had gone through her mind?

That he didn't want anything to do with her.

The thought settled like a rock in his chest. Some instinct he didn't know he had and definitely shouldn't have paid attention to made him seek inside himself for that bright light of the mate bond.

His griffin was sitting curled around it, as though the light was a fire it was trying to warm itself beside. Or as though it was trying to protect it. He'd always thought of mate bonds as sure things, as unbreakable as they were magical, but what if they weren't? What if the mate bond could be broken? Whatever was between them right now felt like a tight string about to snap. If it did—

He reached inside himself and, as gently as he could, touched the glowing light at the center of his soul.

On the sofa, Delphine jumped.

She looked up at him. Too quickly for him to look away.

Their eyes met like a flash fire starting. A shiver went through Hardwick's spine. This was *right*. This was the woman he was meant to be with, and they both knew it. He breathed in, luxuriating in her scent. It didn't even matter that he could only catch glimpses of it, this far across the room. A hint of sweetness, a hint of something wild. The world felt full of possibility.

"What was that?" he murmured.

Delphine went still. If he hadn't been watching her so closely, he wouldn't have noticed it. Nothing about her *changed*. She was still sitting up, poised for action. Her eyes were lit with something that he didn't peg as *hope* until it froze. That look—she—didn't stop, or back down. It was as though she was... waiting.

The moment stretched out.

Delphine licked her lips. "I... thought I spilled my drink," she said. Her glass of water was still safely on the floor beside the sofa, untouched.

Hardwick looked away. Pain shuttled around his skull, starting above his left ear and diving deep behind his eye. He swallowed back a grimace.

When he looked back at Delphine, she was still watching him, a strange look on her face.

Neither of them said anything.

He ran away again while Delphine was doing the dishes. Back into the bedroom and the spiral of his own shame.

He just needed some time alone. *God, please,* he begged silently. His griffin tucked itself into an unhappy ball. All he needed was a week, tops. Then he would be able to think straight.

Just a week.

His head hurt.

And the blizzard was getting worse.

# 13

## DELPHINE

It was like some sort of horrible logic puzzle. If the cabin has three rooms, and one of them is a bathroom and the total size of the building is less than fifty square feet, how long until either Hardwick or Delphine decide to go outside and freeze to death rather than spend another moment in each other's company.

The afternoon crept by. Hardwick emerged from the bedroom to put another frozen pizza in the oven, and the meal that followed was the most awkward dinner she'd experienced since Pebbles brought home her bird of paradise shifter mate.

Hardwick looked after the dishes afterwards. Delphine considered taking a leaf out of his book and hiding in the bedroom until he was done but reconsidered. Over-exposure might be a better cure for how she was feeling than avoidance.

The cabin had a small shelf of well-thumbed books. Louis L'Amour, Dick Francis, a few other authors she'd never heard of whose book covers were promisingly full of suave men with guns and tropical

palms. She grabbed one at random and curled up ·
on the sofa. If she was stuck here until the weather
cleared with a man who couldn't make it more
obvious that he didn't want her around, she could at
least read some good old-fashioned airport novels.

She cracked the book open. It started well.
Someone got murdered, there was an explosion, and
the characters were talking about cell phones like
they were some sort of far-future technology.

Murder... explosion... tech...

It took Delphine ten minutes to realize she'd been
staring at the same page for significantly longer than
ten minutes.

Hardwick was still at the kitchen sink. If he
scrubbed the dishes any harder, there wasn't going
to be anything left.

Hardwick was leaning over the kitchen bench.
His shirt was stretched over his shoulders, outlining
sharp shoulder blades and the lean curve of his back.

She imagined he would look the same if she was
wedged against the bench in front of him. Face
up, kissing him, or face down, straining around to
capture as much of his skin with her lips as she could
as he pinned her down.

It wasn't just her cheeks anymore. Every inch of
her skin was seared with heat.

She glared at her book.

At last he finished. Delphine, who was definitely still reading, tensed.

And Hardwick went straight into the bedroom.

She closed her eyes and bit off a groan.

The blizzard couldn't end soon enough.

She made scones again the next morning. Not so she could sneak some time in the same room as Hardwick before he woke up. Not at all. She just needed to work out some frustration.

Scones were not the perfect thing for working out one's frustrations.

They came out more like bricks than cheesy, flakey delights.

*At least they're a perfect match for the coffee,* she thought glumly.

They ate in silence. Painful, awkward silence. Delphine had never been so aware of being alone inside her own head, not even when she was surrounded by her family.

"If the weather improves—" she began.

"I can take you to a friend's house." Hardwick's eyes were fixed on his plate. "I've been thinking about it. He lives a way out of town, but not too far. You can tell your family that you flew in and stopped there so that you wouldn't risk anyone from town seeing you."

Delphine couldn't believe what she was hearing. And she got the impression Hardwick couldn't believe what he was saying, either. His voice was flat, as though the words were being dragged unwillingly out of him.

"Your friend?" she asked. She'd met most of Pine Valley's shifters the Christmas before.

"Jackson. He's a good man. He'll help you out, I'm sure of it."

"Jackson Gilles?"

When Hardwick nodded, she gave a weak smile. "That's... perfect. I work for his father, so it all fits together... perfectly."

Except for the bit where she was leaving him.

She coughed. Something in her chest fluttered, and for a moment, just behind her eyes, she saw something like a flickering candlelight. She blinked rapidly until it went away.

Across the table, Hardwick's frown had deepened. He rubbed his chest with a grimace. "What a coincidence."

"He's the one who brought me to Pine Valley in the first place." *If he hadn't...*

"Great. Let's keep that plan in mind, then." He stood up to clear the table. "I didn't sleep well last night, so don't worry about me being in your hair today."

"Sure." Delphine put so much effort into not imagining Hardwick sleeping in the bed she'd tossed and turned in all night that she didn't put as much tact into her next words as she might have: "Can I borrow some clothes?"

"Can you—"

Hardwick looked right at her for the first time that morning. His already dark eyes seemed even blacker than she remembered. His mouth opened as if he was about to sleep and Delphine's eyes were drawn to it. Had his lips been that chapped yesterday? The shadows under his eyes had been less deep, she knew that. And the exhaustion weighing down his shoulders less heavy.

The rush of heat that had poured through her when she locked eyes with Hardwick faded away. It was replaced by a surge of guilt.

He'd told her he needed this time to recuperate from his work. And yet here she was, destroying his solitude, eating into his vacation time, and feeding him a terrible breakfast. He'd even figured out a way that she could return to town without giving her family anything to be suspicious about.

She needed to fix this.

Hardwick loaned her an extra outfit. She showered, if that was the right word for it, in what was little more than a bucket with a tap above it in the bathroom and shivered into the borrowed sweatpants and t-shirt. She would have to heat some water on the stove to handwash her own clothes.

But that was a problem to solve later.

Hardwick.

She'd been off-footed ever since she woke up here. No, that was a lie—hah. A lie she wouldn't have even noticed before she met him.

In truth, she'd been off her game since well before Hardwick rescued her. Before the crash, too. Even before she had arrived in Pine Valley, ready to prep Mr. Petrakis's vacation rental so it would be ready when he arrived.

It had started the year before, when her work took her to this tiny mountain town and another Christmas away from her family, and she'd woken up one morning to discover that her mother and brothers had come to meet her for the holiday.

Away from the rest of the Belgrave clan. Away from Grandfather's ironclad declarations about what Belgraves were meant to be. Away from Grandmother's flinty eyes that saw far too much, and Aunt Grizelda's endless stories about their glorious history. It had been just the four of them, together, for the first time since Delphine had left home.

And she'd acted exactly the same way with them as she had with the wider family.

Maybe there was nothing left of her *except* her lies.

She splashed water on her face. It was cold, but not chilly enough to take the burn of shame from her cheeks. She filled the tiny, chipped sink and let her hands rest in the water until they were cold, then laid them over her face.

She didn't regret what she had done. All those years of lies. How could she? The results spoke for themselves. The Belgrave clan had never been more harmonious.

But now that Pebbles and her mate were married...

Delphine shook her head.

That was a problem to solve later, too. Her problem, right now, was how she was going to manage however much time there was left before the storm ended.

Wind howled around the cabin as though it had heard her and wanted her to know how very long that time would be. She groaned and pressed her hands against her eyes.

*I'll manage*, she told herself silently. Big surprise, she wasn't convinced. Not listening to the voices in her head was just another sign that she was a failed shifter, she thought with a sigh, even if the only voice there was her own.

This was nothing new. It was also a pain in the arse. If she ever wanted to really talk herself into something, she had to actually *talk* herself into it. This wasn't a problem when she was at work, mostly because Mr. Petrakis rarely listened to what anyone else was saying unless they were saying his name. But here? Now? With a man who could sense lies in the next room?

A gorgeous man, she thought. The sort of man who would have turned her head even if she'd met him in a crowded room and not in a place where he was the only other person in the room. A man with a restrained, intense energy that was strangely compelling. Hell, he was a griffin shifter who could literally sense lies. She should have been doing everything she could to keep out of his way. Instead, she wanted... she wanted...

She shook her head. What she wanted, as usual, didn't matter. What she *should* do was what she always did: keep the peace. Usually she kept the peace between her boss and his colleagues, or her family and other members of her family, but she could keep the peace between herself and Hardwick, too. Surely.

That plan felt like solid ground.

All she needed to do was figure out what would make him the least upset that she was stuck here with him and bend herself into shape until she could make it happen.

She wished she could bend herself around—

Nope. Thinking like that wasn't going to help anything. Not that, she discovered with a thrill of surprise, she was averse to a holiday hook-up. At least not when it came to Hardwick. But the way he'd glared at her through all of their conversations so far didn't exactly suggest he would be interested in that.

"Pity," she murmured.

Or maybe not. Getting involved with a man who could sense lies, even temporarily, was probably a bad idea.

Something in her chest fluttered and she rubbed it absently.

First things first, she should probably not look like a total nutcase when she went back out there. She checked herself in the tiny mirror again.

"Like a half-drowned rat," she muttered to herself, and combed her fingers through her hair. With her hair tucked neatly behind her ears and her face patted dry, she looked almost presentable.

She placed her hands either side of the sink and stared hard at herself. "You can do this," she told herself, keeping her voice low enough that she hoped Hardwick wouldn't be able to hear her, even with his super-sensitive shifter hearing. "It's only for a few days. Just until the weather clears."

Was that a lie, she wondered? Did it count as a lie if she couldn't look into the future and know if she was right or not?

She'd never asked herself this sort of question before. There was a sort of sinking feeling in her stomach when she realized she'd never really considered whether anything she did or said was a lie or not. All that had mattered was whether it would help her keep up her pretense that she was a shifter like the rest of her family.

Her shoulders tightened. Only long years of experience stopped them from hunching up defensively.

Irritated, Delphine took a deep breath and looked herself in the eye. The only person that looked back was herself. Human, tired, and frustrated.

Those last two sounded a lot like Hardwick.

Her frown deepened as she thought about him. She forced her mind away from the parts of him it had been focusing on the most, and concentrated on the—

The tells, she realized with a start. Those little, unconscious tics that she'd tried so hard to iron out from her own expressions and reactions.

His grim, set expression. The lines that sat so deeply around his mouth and between his eyebrows they might have been carved there. The way his eyelid flickered sometimes, or he pulled back, a movement that might have looked like a flinch if it wasn't so… slow, and controlled… as though it was something he was used to. Something that happened all the time. Like watching a ball come towards you and knowing you weren't going to be able to get out of the way in time, so you just watch it coming and think, Shit, this is going to hurt.

All the little things she'd observed about him bumped together in her head, forming a whole that made her eyes widen. If she was right…

She wasn't Hardwick's mate. She knew that. But maybe, if she was right about this, she could make herself useful. Make him a bit less miserable, since it was her fault she was stuck here, ruining his solo trip.

And the first step of that was going out and facing him. Or at least being in the same room as him, which was just as nerve-wracking.

She glared at herself in the mirror.

"Come on," she urged herself. "You can do this. You're a real Belgrave, damn it!"

In the next room, something crashed to the floor.

Delphine yanked the bathroom door open. Hardwick was still over by the stove. He was leaning over, one hand clutching his head. A baking tray was lying on the floor, with two frozen meals scattered next to it.

She felt hot and cold all over. He looked as though a sudden headache had caught him just as he was about to put the meal in the oven. At the same moment as she had said…

She gulped.

Was her theory correct?

And if it was, did that mean…

# 14

# HARDWICK

Hardwick swore as he waited for the pain to subside. It lingered longer, this time, clinging like wet kelp to the inside of his skull.

It was getting worse. Like an allergy that got more dangerous the more you were exposed to the allergen.

How long had he tried to ignore that inconvenient fact?

*Long enough to get your partner hurt.*

Guilt burned at the back of his throat. A year and a half ago, he'd been on stakeout with Jackson Gilles—a drug bust. It should have been simple, especially with one officer who could sort truth from fiction in the blink of an eye. They'd done it before. Hundreds of times.

And this time, Hardwick messed up, and Jackson paid the price.

He hadn't realized how exhausted he was until it was too late to pull out of the mission. His skull had felt like it was about to crack, and there had been a permanent buzz in his ears that no amount of caffeine could shake. Jackson had trusted Hardwick to let him know when a situation was about to go bad, but he'd been too out of it. He missed his mark, and Jackson almost took a bullet to the head.

The shot had grazed his forehead, right above his eyebrow. He'd dropped like it had killed him. It was the biggest mistake Hardwick had ever made.

Was he making another mistake, right now?

He rubbed his forehead and knelt down to clean up the mess.

"Hardwick?"

Shit.

Delphine was standing in the doorway. Her hair was damp around the sides of his face, as though she'd splashed it under the tap. That sounded like a damned good idea. Maybe if he stuck his face in an ice bucket, he could freeze his headache away.

"Are you okay?" Delphine asked.

Hardwick scraped frozen vegetables back onto the baking tray and straightened. "Yeah, I just—"

White flashed across his vision as he straightened. His griffin hissed, clawing at its beak. Shit, he wasn't usually this thoughtless. Lying out loud, when he was still waiting to get over the last hit?

"You just don't look so great." Suddenly, Delphine was at his side, both hands under his elbow. She detached the baking tray from his paralyzed grip and tugged him, not completely gently, over to the sofa. "Is it a migraine?"

"Headache."

"Glass of water?"

He nodded, which made his head throb even worse, and could barely force himself to look up when Delphine returned a moment later with a glass of ice-cold water. She looked pale.

"Does this… happen a lot?"

"Worse this time of year," he gritted out, and sipped on the water. Maybe if he tipped it over his head…

"Would you like a massage?"

He blinked. "A what?"

"A…" Her cheeks went a shade of pink that made him want to touch them. "A massage? If it's a tension headache, it could help."

It could help. But… hell. Just the thought of her touching him like that made his griffin want to roll over and beg.

"Sure," his mouth said before his brain could tell it what a bad idea it was.

Delphine got him to lay back along the sofa, with his head propped on the arm. He closed his eyes and took a deep breath, and still jumped when she touched him.

"Sorry," she said at once, and he grumbled something that was meant to be somewhere between

'Don't worry about it' and 'My fault,' and ended up sounding more like an angry bear woken up halfway through hibernation. To his surprise, Delphine took it in her stride.

She let her fingers rest gently either side of his face. Just the fingertips, but each point of connection seemed to glow. Her fingers were cool, and Hardwick couldn't repress a groan as she ran them along his scalp. She found every gnarled rope of tension he hadn't even known was there, from his temples to behind his ears and at the base of his skull. Her touch moved seamlessly from gentle and soothing to firm enough to dig into rock-like knots.

He'd had physical therapy before, but it was nothing like this.

It was incredible. Completely professional, and at the same time almost unbearably, toe-curlingly sensual.

He'd thought that was a figure of speech. Toes curling because something was so good. Thank God he was wearing indoor shoes.

His griffin was in heaven. To it, all of this was right. Even when he reminded it that being close to Delphine was a sure ticket to hurt, it kept trying to gaze lovingly at her through his eyes.

Hardwick kept his eyes shut. Letting her look after him like this might mean less hurt now, but it was as good as a promise for more hurt later.

He groaned again as she got him to tip his head to one side and ran her thumb along the tense cord of his neck. "Where did you learn how to do this?"

The question was a rookie mistake. She hadn't lied to him since she'd seen him drop the meal—because she'd been busy asking questions. Make her answer one of her own, and he had no doubt she'd slip back into the lies that seemed like her natural way of being.

And she would feel him tense under her fingers and know that he couldn't just sense her lies. They hurt him.

He couldn't say why he didn't want her to know that. Probably some sort of masculine dislike of appearing weak. Frankly, he wasn't in the mood for that sort of self-introspection right now.

Her embarrassed chuckle took him by surprise. She rested her hands on his shoulders for a moment before beginning to massage them.

"It was a work thing," she admitted. And it *was* an admission. It was the truth. "A professional development course for personal assistants."

"You do this for your boss?" His eyes flew open. He was about to sit up and put an end to the stolen moment of connection when she tipped her head back and gave a gurgling laugh.

"No! No, that would... absolutely not." She snorted, unladylike for the first time since they had met. His heart thudded. "I thought the course was some sort of mental self-improvement thing for dealing with difficult managers, and then they brought out the scented oils. The whole thing was like something straight out of the 1950s. Deal with your boss by giving him some personal stress-relief after his busy day being a big, important man."

Hardwick didn't trust himself to say anything to that, so he kept his mouth shut.

"I told Mr. Petrakis it was a course on mental resilience, or something. I can't remember what. And filtered all of the company's follow-up emails to a special spam folder all of their very own." Her fingers dug into the base of his skull again and stayed there until his head relaxed back, supported by her hands. "I told myself it might come in handy one day, at least... and here we are."

It was the longest she'd spoken to him without setting off explosions in his head. His griffin was drunk on her laughter, and he found himself letting go of the wariness he'd clung to since she first woke up. He even forgot about the wavering light in his heart. For a few minutes, they weren't stalking around each other, stepping over unsaid secrets like prowling cats.

He talked about his work. Not the mistake with Jackson, but the bigger picture. Using his ability to help get criminals off the street.

"Not that it's only criminals who lie," he found himself saying. "Everyone does. And they all think they have a reason for it."

"Even your colleagues?"

He thought of Jackson again. His partner was the non-shifter son of two shifter parents. He'd acted like he didn't care, but there'd always been a halo of untruth around it. Like when he said he'd left Pine Valley only for his career, and not because a girl had broken his heart.

He was back with the girl now, though. Hardwick had left town too quickly to hear the story behind that change of heart.

But Jackson's lies hadn't hurt that much. Nor had anyone else. Not until the mistake.

"Colleagues, sure. When no one wants to own up to leaving their moldy coffee cups under their desks." Among other things.

He stole a glance at Delphine. Her eyes were firmly on her work, but she was frowning.

"How do you—" she began, and then bit her lip. "How does that feel now?" she asked, and he couldn't shake the feeling she'd been about to say something else.

He stretched his head from side to side. "Better."

"I'll just finish up, then." She gently pushed his head back to center. "Let me know if I'm rubbing too hard. Like I said, this is meant to be a scented-oil thing."

"Wasn't planning on it being that sort of vacation," Hardwick said before he could stop himself.

"Hah!" Another surprise. Hardwick had barely even gotten started reprimanding himself when Delphine let out a bark of laughter. Her fingers shook. When she smoothed them across his forehead, it was as though she was trying to smooth out her own chuckles as well. "Close your eyes," she said, and he did.

His griffin tapped its beak, staring sadly at the darkness behind his eyelids. Hardwick relaxed into the sensation of Delphine's hands on him. He left his griffin pining, and, almost feeling guilty, checked on the light of the mate-bond in his heart.

It didn't flare, or sparkle, or anything else dramatic. But its glow was stronger. It barely flickered at all as he watched it.

*It will hurt more later,* he reminded himself. There were too many complications. He'd meant what he said about everyone thinking they had a reason for lying. It didn't matter how much his heart glowed for Delphine; he couldn't do this now. He couldn't afford the time it would take him to unravel her reasons. Not when every attempt would turn into the migraine from hell.

He knew he was an asshole when his head started playing up. Better he not say anything than dig too deep and lash out at her when his investigation only got him more lies.

"One more thing…" Delphine rested her fingertips on his forehead, just above his eyebrows. "It doesn't hurt you when I lie. Does it."

Not a question. A statement.

A knife to the center of his forehead.

# 15

# DELPHINE

The moment she lied, Hardwick flinched. The tension she'd eased from his forehead slammed back. If she had her hands on his neck or shoulders, she was sure she would have felt the knots she'd worked so hard to get rid of come back with a vengeance.

And she hated herself for it.

She'd needed to know, she told herself. If she was going to figure out what was going on with him, and *help* him, she needed proof that he couldn't just sense lies. They *hurt* him.

She'd hurt him.

She'd been hurting him since the moment she woke up.

Her lungs suddenly couldn't fill properly. She stepped back and her hands clenched into fists. She was horrified—at herself, at everything she'd so casually lied to him about, at the cruel test she'd just put him through. And that horror turned into anger.

How *dare* he not tell her that she was hurting him. They were stuck out here together, in the middle of nowhere. He'd *saved her life*. She had wanted to find some way of making the situation less awkward and awful for the both of them, and his plan had been to sit there for as long as they were stuck together, and let her hurt him?

What sort of a person did that?

Her chest felt as though it was about to burst. Hardwick swung his legs around and stood up. He wasn't moving as though every action made his head throb anymore—he was all controlled strength and wary grace. So compelling her mouth went dry. She wanted—she wanted—

"What the hell was that?" he growled. The look on his face wasn't angry, though. He looked betrayed.

Her heart twisted.

"What was *that*?" she replied. She wasn't even angry at him, she told herself as her voice turned into a snarl. She was angry at herself. At her grandparents. At this whole twisted, horrible world. "What about telling me the truth?"

He flinched back. Surprise, not pain. "The truth?"

"Your powers. You don't just *sense* lies, do you? They hurt you. I've been hurting you."

Hardwick ran one hand over his mouth. She couldn't read the expression in his eyes. "You're right."

"Why didn't you say anything?"

"It wasn't important—"

"We're stuck out here together, and it *wasn't important?*" She clutched her head, then her chest, not knowing what she was doing. "You're not just here for a vacation, you're—you're *detoxing.*"

He nodded.

"And I'm about as tox as it gets."

All her rage faded away, so quickly she still didn't know who or what it had been aimed at.

"In that case, I'm even sorrier that you've been landed with me," she muttered.

"I thought you deserved a break."

She shot him a confused look. "A break from what?"

"You said your family would be happier if you didn't get in touch." Hardwick's voice was low and even. He sounded as though he was reading off of notes. She wondered if this was the voice he used in his job, trying to get suspects to admit their stories weren't straight. "If there's something going on, if your family is hurting you, there are—"

"My family isn't *hurting* me!"

Hardwick winced.

No. No, that hadn't been a lie. Her family *weren't* hurting her. Because she'd figured out how to stop that from happening. That was the whole point of—

"It's nothing like that," she said quickly, which was a neat, tidy cover-all, especially if she didn't specify what *that* was. She ran her fingers through her hair.

"What is it like, then?"

"It's—"

Complicated. Too much a part of her life for her to peel off and talk about like it was something separate, like it wasn't *her*.

"—not my story to tell. Not all of it," she said at last. "But I'm not—I'm doing it to stop other people from being hurt. Like I don't want to hurt you. Nobody's hurting me."

Hardwick grimaced and put one hand to his forehead. "That's not true."

"I just told you, my family—"

"I'm not talking about them."

Regret clawed at his features, making him look older than he was. "You must have guessed. You must have felt something. You're right about lies hurting me, but I can't blame you for hurting me when I've been doing the same to you since we met."

"You haven't—" Her heart thrummed in her chest. Her cheeks were hot. "I d-don't know what you're talking about."

"My power hurting me isn't the only thing you suspect me of hiding, is it?"

"You—" Delphine cut herself off and went completely still.

# 16

# HARDWICK

Hardwick was acting like an ass. He knew that. He'd been acting like one since the moment he woke up, alone and wretched on the sofa.

But he wanted to hear her say it. Not for any bullshit macho reason. This wasn't a power play, or some sort of twisted game.

He just needed to hear her tell the truth. Needed it like he needed to breathe, or eat, or for his heart to keep on beating. Looking at her now, her face like a mask, he felt as though he'd opened his heart and was about to have it crushed.

"I understand why you didn't say anything. You've been watching me, figuring me out, and I think I figured a few things about you, too. You're a non-shifter who lives among shifters and you have to convince them you're one of them. You're always watching. You can't trust your own senses because they're not the right senses: you can't send or hear telepathic messages; you can't shift. You can't even meet their eyes, in case they look inside you and all they see is human," he added, remembering the way her eyes danced away from his after that first, wonderful moment of connection. "The only way you can know what people are saying, with words you can't hear, is by waiting for their reactions. Body language, expressions, vocalizations... Like my griffin. A whole different language that they don't even know they're speaking."

He took a step closer to her.

"You probably don't even trust your own senses anymore."

She leaned towards him, her feet rooted to the ground.

"Not your normal senses."

"I don't have any other sort," she whispered, and he couldn't tell whether the thudding in his skull was new or the same baseline pain. Perhaps she didn't know, either.

He stopped. He wanted to reach out to her, lay it all out, give her the framework she so clearly relied on and let her build her story on top of it—but he didn't only want to reach out to her.

He wanted her to reach out to him, too.

She licked her lips.

"You're right," she said.

*True.* His griffin crooned relief.

"I can't trust senses I don't have. I have to guess—educated guesses, but I don't always get it right. And that's with things I know. People I know.

I can pass it off as a misunderstanding, mostly, or let them think that I wasn't paying attention or didn't care enough to be listening to them, but it's never… never anything important. I make sure of that. If there was… something important… and I felt something new, something I didn't understand…"

Her hand fluttered to her chest again.

"How could I believe it?"

"Trust yourself," Hardwick urged her. "Stop thinking about what you ought to do and trust what your heart wants."

"I could hurt—"

"I don't care if you hurt me," he said. "I thought I did. I thought I could push you away until I was better, but I've just made it worse."

Her hand flew to her chest. "I don't know what you—"

A flash of pain across his forehead. She gasped.

"Please," he whispered, and her mask slipped.

Delphine clenched her fists. He got the feeling she would have looked away from him if she could, but her eyes were fixed on his.

"You feel it, too?" she asked, her voice cracking. Before he could reply, she made a sharp, negating gesture with her hand. "No, don't—don't answer that. I have to do this. I *want* to."

She took a hesitant step forward. "I wasn't going to say anything. I never do. Not unless I'm absolutely sure." The corner of her mouth twitched. "So I'd better be sure."

She darted forward and slipped her hands around his neck. Before Hardwick could react, her lips were pressed against his.

And the spark that had flickered to life inside him when he first saw her burst into flame.

# 17

## DELPHINE

O h, God.

This was *real.*

Delphine had never experienced magic. The itch of knowing someone was trying to speak to her telepathically didn't count. It was just a reminder of what she couldn't do.

She'd *seen* magic—seen her brothers and parents transform into mythical animals, seen them communicate without speaking, seen them fly golden and shining in front of burning sunsets. But she'd never had any of her own.

Was this magic?

Doubt curled through her, even as Hardwick pulled her closer and kissed her back. The light that flickered inside her burst into glorious flame. But that had to be a hallucination. Her mind was playing tricks on her. How could she see light flaring in her chest when her eyes were closed? It was—

It was—

Real.

All the tension she'd been holding in her back and shoulders released. She melted against Hardwick, pressing the soft curved of her body into the hard lines of his. He softened, too, wrapping himself around her and kissing her until she gasped for breath.

He lifted his head.

Her eyes fluttered open.

Hardwick's face was only inches from hers. She breathed in and inhaled his unique scent of whatever I said it was earlier. Earthy and magical at the same time. Perfect. *Him.*

His eyes stared directly into hers. She was no stranger to this by now. They'd spent long enough glaring at each other. But she'd never seen him with this look in his eyes: soft and gentle, and strangely vulnerable.

He started to pull away; she held him tight.

All the words she'd stopped herself from saying the day before, the words that had whirled around her head as she lay in bed trying to sleep and trying not to think of Hardwick sleeping or not sleeping in the next room, came out in a rush.

"I wasn't going to say anything. I was going to leave..."

"I know." Regret tightened Hardwick's mouth. "I was, too."

"I was afraid—"

"Yes," he sighed, and his sigh took her heart with it. This was it. She was afraid, and she was a liar, and she wasn't good enough. Not good enough to be a proper Belgrave, and not good enough to be his. "I was afraid, too."

*What?*

"What did you have to be afraid of?"

"Myself." He closed his eyes and rested his forehead against hers. "The two of us, together. I'm... complicated... and with my griffin's powers, things are so black and white. You need someone who can handle complexity. Someone who—"

"Don't say it."

"Someone easier than me."

She hissed a curse and dug her fingers into his hair, pulling his head back to look him in the eyes. "We'll make it work," she told him. "We'll find a way. I promise. It doesn't have to be complicated."

She tensed, waiting for the wince that would betray her lie.

It never came.

Hardwick must have been waiting, too. His eyes widened. "Delphine—"

Whatever he was about to say, she never heard it. She kissed him again, pressing her whole body against him until he stumbled backwards.

Her skin was electric. Hardwick put one hand around her waist, steadying them both, and the sensation took all the breath from her lungs. His other hand went to her cheek, the line of her jaw, cupped the back of her head as he deepened the kiss. His tongue flicked against her lips and she opened her mouth, desire a sharp pull inside her.

He lifted his head. "Are you sure now?"

Delphine nodded. There were no words for how sure she was. So other words came up, instead.

"How did you know that I don't do what I want? I don't even know what I want, half the time."

"I guessed." He pressed his forehead against hers. "When you let slip that your family didn't know you weren't a shifter. I thought, there was no way you could *want* to do that all the time. And once you start building your life around one thing like that, once you start putting your own desires behind whatever grand plan you came up with… Of course you'd get confused."

He understood her. She should have been terrified. Instead, she melted.

"You weren't, though. Confused. You knew straight away?"

"From the moment I saw you." There was a growl in his voice that made all the hairs on the back of her neck stand on end. He raised one hand to cup the back of her head, then dragged it down, smoothing the hairs as though he knew what effect his voice had had.

But he hadn't said anything. Because—

"From the moment I started hurting you," she corrected him.

No wince. No grimace of pain. Just a flicker of guilt in the depths of his eyes. Was she seeing him, or his griffin?

Delphine breathed in. Hardwick was all his particular smells, wild and magical, strange and *home* at the same time. She wanted—God, she wanted—

"Tell me," he breathed, and the growl didn't stop at her neck this time; it traveled down her body, prickling and enticing, bringing parts of her to life she'd almost given up for dead. "Tell me when you first sensed something between us,"

"From the moment I saw you," she admitted. "Sitting there, watching me. I should have been dead—"

"No."

"I would have been dead. And then I was alive, and you were there, and I felt..."

She kissed him again. She couldn't help it. The day she'd spent fighting her feelings had stretched her out like a bowstring, and now that it was released there was no way she could fight any longer.

"I know what I want now," she whispered against his lips. "I want you."

Hardwick's arms tightened around her. The hand at the back of her neck held her more firmly, keeping her in place. Where she belonged. Oh, God, how could she have doubted this?

"Say it again," he growled.

"I want you."

Hardwick groaned. She tensed, thinking she'd said something wrong, hurt him again—but when she tore her lips from his and stared into his eyes, they were shining and dark, the difference between his pupils and irises barely visible.

"Again," he whispered, trailing his hand over her jaw. "Tell me something else true."

*Something else true.* The thrill of it took her breath away. It felt wrong, somehow. Wicked. It was so opposite to everything she'd built around herself, and so dangerous. To tell the truth was to reveal part of herself she kept hidden even from herself.

"I want you to kiss me—"

He kissed her, his fingers tangling in her hair. She wriggled against him.

"No—here—"

She indicated with her fingers. First her jawline. Then her neck. The thick muscle at the top of her shoulder, then the sensitive skin over her collarbone. She pulled at her clothing. "There—"

He trailed a line of kisses down her chest. Each touch made her bite back a moan until his mouth landed on her breast and she gave in. A shuddering sigh escaped her as he dragged her bra down and kissed her nipple.

"Oh, God—teeth —"

"I'll be gentle."

"No—I want—"

Hardwick's growl of understanding was almost as incredible as the sensation of his teeth scraping against her nipple. He bit her—gently, then harder, as she gasped with pleasure. The pain twisted inside her, joining with the strange, vulnerable wrong-right-ness of telling him what she wanted. Her fingers dug into his shoulders.

"I want you to take your clothes off."

Hardwick looked up at her. His dark eyes flashed, and he straightened, reluctant, but cheeks flushed with desire.

"No!" she burst out as he pulled on the hem of his shirt. "I want to do it."

He let out a bark of surprised laughter. "You don't know what you want."

"I do." She grabbed at his shirt. She felt light-headed. "I just keep changing my mind about how to get it."

"Oh?"

His smile was one Delphine had never seen before. Slow and sly and intimate. It fit his face so much better than the wary scowl she was used to. She kissed him, bunching her hands in his shirt. "You should do that more often."

"Do what?"

"Look at me like that."

He let out a ragged breath. "Delphine—"

She pulled his shirt up. He raised his arms, helping her drag the shirt over his head. She didn't notice where it went. His chest was hot, so hot, his heartbeat strong under her fingers.

And he was just really fucking sexy to look at.

"I love your body."

Hardwick's breath caught in his throat. She looked up at him, her fingertips dancing lower. "You told me to tell the truth."

"I didn't realize I'd be letting the dam loose." He caught her fingers and kissed them. "Don't stop."

She couldn't even if she wanted to.

"I want you to take my shirt off."

His fingers ghosted alone her spine, the calluses sending shockwaves across her skin.

"Kiss my neck."

His arms twined around her, lifting her off the ground as she fumbled with his trouser zipper.

"Touch me—"

She was his mate. That was miracle enough. That he listened to her every shameless, whispered plea, and obeyed, his eyes black with desire and his breath hot on her skin? It shouldn't have been possible.

Nothing she wanted so much should have been possible.

She slipped one hand under the band of his briefs. His hips bucked, fingers tightening almost painfully around her waist as she wrapped her hand around his cock.

He was hard. That shouldn't have been a surprise. What surprised her was the thrill that went through her as she felt him in her hand, thick and urgent and wanting.

She kissed him until he moaned and pumped her hand up and down his cock until whatever words he'd been about to say came out in a jumbled gasp against her lips. "What was that?"

"I can't take this much longer." He jerked against her again. "God, Delphine…"

She stripped her pants off one-handed. He slid his hands over her ass, pulling her up so she could wrap her legs around him. His cock pressed between her legs, sending shivers of anticipation into her core. She ground against him.

"Bed?" she suggested.

"Is that what you want?"

Somehow, through the very determined messages her body was sending her and the messages his body was sending her, too, she sensed the hesitation in his voice.

"Honestly?"

"Honestly," he breathed, easily, as though her voice had never made him double over in pain.

"Honestly, I'm easy on where."

That smile again. He picked her up and she kissed the side of his neck, his earlobe, wherever she could reach until he put her down next to the sofa.

"Here?" she asked.

"Last night—" He cleared his throat, embarrassment mingling with desire. She leaned against the back of the sofa and put his arms around his neck, keeping him close.

"Tell me," she whispered. "Fair turnabout."

He acknowledged her point with a quick smile. "Sleeping here last night, knowing you were just in the next room, surrounded by your scent all over the cushions and the blanket... it was hell."

"You didn't sleep well either?"

"You too?"

"I didn't even get to smell your scent on the bed," she grumbled.

"I hadn't slept there yet."

He pushed her against the back of the sofa, kissing her deeply. "Let's change that," she whispered.

Hardwick picked her up and was about to lay her down on the sofa, but she wriggled out of his grasp. She didn't know why. This was wrong-right and exciting and everything she wanted, and what she wanted was—

She almost groaned with the arguing *wants* inside her. She wanted now. Here. Everything. All the years she'd spent bottling herself up meant there was so much she'd *never* tried.

She could start here. *They* could start here.

"No. Here," she said, turning around so that she was leaning over the sofa, Hardwick pressed hard against her back. His cock jutted against her ass. "Please?"

His hands slid onto her hips. "This is what you want?"

"Yes—"

"Tell me."

"I want you to take me. Like this. Hard. *Please.*"

His fingers dug into the soft flesh of her waist. He kissed the back of her neck and she twisted so she could capture his lips with hers. She bit him—gently. Hard enough that his cock jumped.

"You're incredible," he breathed. "I never thought—"

"*Please,*" she begged, and his words dissolved into a low chuckle.

"As my lady wishes."

He slid one hand down between her legs and parted her folds. Delphine bucked, despite herself; it was so long since anyone had touched her like this. And Hardwick was like no one else she'd ever been with. He pushed one finger inside her.

Delphine moaned. It felt so good, but... "That's not enough," she complained.

"I don't want to hurt you."

Still riding high on sensation and the wonder of the light burning in her chest, she didn't stop to wonder why the next words that came out of her mouth were: "I don't care. Hurt me. Anything. *Please.*"

Hardwick growled something wordless against her shoulder. She gasped as he removed his finger and repositioned himself, both hands back around her waist. She reached back and wrapped one hand around his cock, guiding him into place.

The head of his cock nudged between her legs. Delphine bit her lip. This was happening. This was all really, truly happening. To *her.*

"Yes," she whispered, and he thrust forward.

Her back arched as he pushed inside her to the hilt. His cock was thick, she knew that—but to have it all inside her, all at once, to *feel* it, was something else entirely. She'd gone onto tip-toes automatically, her body so surprised by the sudden intrusion, but Hardwick held her down. He nuzzled into her shoulder, soft words that made her melt against him.

Then he started to move his hips, and Delphine groaned.

Small movements. Tiny. The merest suggestion of a thrust, retreat, thrust again. But Delphine felt each one as though it was a lightning strike. The pleasure building inside her was so intense she thought she would go limp, but instead she strained backwards, pressing against him, desperate to wring more sensation out of every aggravatingly small movement.

"Not enough for you?" Hardwick teased. Hardwick. *Teased*. The newness of it shot through her and she laughed.

"Do I need to tell you?" she asked, twining one leg around his. Opening herself more for him.

"Always." His voice was rough. Delphine flexed her leg, holding him tight against her. His heartbeat thundered against her back; she could feel every breath he took, deep and ragged. The hand she'd used to guide his cock to her entrance was trapped between them, fingers spread out against his abs.

"Then please," she asked, her own voice catching. "I want you to fuck me hard."

He kissed the side of her jaw, then pulled back and drove into her so hard she lost her breath. Before she could catch it, he fucked into her again. She cried out, her one free hand scrambling on the sofa back to keep herself upright. She tried to pull the other one free to help steady herself and he grabbed it.

Hardwick locked her hand in place, not letting her move an inch as he thrust into her.

Whatever it was that telling the truth about she wanted had unleashed inside her, it had done the same to him. He whispered gentle, soft praise in her ear as he drove into her again and again, his words completely at odds with the brute force of every thrust.

Pressure built up inside her. Every time he filled her, she thought it would be too much, too hard, too overwhelming—and every time he pulled back it was too soon, leaving her crying out for more. His fingers dug into her hip, the nails scratching, and she keened as the pain arced deep inside her.

"Did you like that?" Wonder threaded through his voice.

Delphine made a noise that she hoped he read as *yes, yes, fucking hell yes.* She twisted her tongue around a few words, hoping they would come out right. "Did you?"

"Did I enjoy—" He thrust into her. "Hearing you make a noise—" Again. "Like that?"

He buried his face in the corner of her neck. "Yes."

His teeth scratched her skin. "Do you want this?"

"Y-yes." That had come out too uncertain. She licked her lips. "Yes, Hardwick, please—"

He bit down. Delphine gasped, then moaned as he released her, kissing and licking where it hurt.

When he thrust into her again, he bit down, too, and the pain shot straight to the stretched, full feeling inside her, and Hardwick's grip on her waist and her trapped hand. It all tangled up with the feeling of being held down and asking for what she wanted and getting it, and what she wanted being what he wanted, too, and all built up inside her.

She came so hard her legs collapsed beneath her. If not for Hardwick's arm around her she would have collapsed over the sofa, helpless as her body clenched and throbbed around his cock. He groaned into her neck and thrust into her again, and her already sparking nerve endings exploded again. She arched against him, legs trembling, words pouring from her mouth—"Oh, God, Hardwick, please don't stop, please—"and he came inside her, his cock pumping as he wrapped his arms more tightly around her.

They stood together, half-collapsed, holding one another as their breathing slowed. Delphine grasped for Hardwick's hand on her waist and wound her fingers through his. He lifted their joined hands to her chest.

"It's changed," he whispered, his voice ragged. "Do you feel it?"

She didn't need to ask what he meant. She didn't even need to close her eyes to see that the bright light inside her heart was glowing even stronger than it had after their first kiss. And it wasn't just a lonely star. Part of it stretched out, a ribbon of golden light that stretched from her heart to Hardwick's.

"I can feel it," she gasped. "I can—I can *see* it. But how is that possible? It's inside me..."

"My griffin is inside me, but I can see it." Hardwick brushed a strand of her hair back and turned her head to kiss her. "I don't know whether you call it your mind's eye, or seeing into your own soul, but the way I see my griffin and the way I see our bond is the same."

*Our bond.*

Delphine was suddenly aware of the world slotting back into existence around her. The warm cabin filled only with the sounds of their breathing and the gentle fire-noises of the stove. Outside, the heavy silence of snow and the mountains. And then, somewhere beyond that...

The real world.

Her family.

And the old her, her old self, the one she'd built so carefully.

Something inside her snapped shut, afraid.

# 18

## HARDWICK

Delphine went stiff in his arms.

"Are you cold?" he asked, reluctantly slipping out of her. She half-turned, one hand still clasping his, the other rising to rest on his chest. "We can move to the bed now if you like."

"It's not that. I—" She looked up at him, her face pinched. "What happens now?"

He reached for the mate bond. His parents had told him once that they could use it to communicate even more closely than they could with telepathy. Telepathy could send words, but two mated shifters could send emotions down their mate bond.

But not him, apparently. When he tried to hold onto the mate bond it slipped out of his psychic grasp, as immaterial as mist.

Was it because Delphine wasn't a shifter?

His jaw tightened. Thank goodness she *couldn't* feel his emotions, because that stray thought might have just broken her.

"Now?" he said out loud, trying to push away the guilt and worry building up inside him. "It's almost Christmas—"

He didn't need a mate bond to see the sudden panic in her eyes. Thank all the stars she was finally being honest with him, and not hiding her genuine responses behind her mask of lies.

"You don't want to go back to your family for Christmas, do you?"

Delphine opened her mouth. Shut it again. Gave him a look that told him this probably wasn't a conversation to be had in a naked clinch.

He tugged her towards her and kissed her forehead. "Tell you what. Let's get cleaned up. I'll put on some food. You can tell me later—"

Her shoulders stiffened.

"—if you want."

He let her have the bathroom first and grabbed a couple of frozen lasagnas. One veggie, one classic. That was a balanced meal, right, if they split them?

As he heard the shower start to run, he sighed. His shoulders slumped.

Had this all been a terrible idea?

Staying apart from her had been agony. But being with her would be agony, too. She knew now that her lies caused him actual, physical pain, and she seemed to regret it—but now that the glow of their first time together was fading, his headache was back. The dull, constant ache he'd come to think of as all Delphine.

She might want to change. He would believe that. Believe in the *want*, anyway. He'd been on the force too long to fool himself that *want* lasted any time at all against the other pressures in anyone's life. Whatever pressures had caused her to be the way she was, being with him was unlikely to remove them.

She would keep being her. And he would keep hurting—or have to force himself to be apart from her, which would hurt in a different way, but just as badly.

The mood thickened as Delphine borrowed more of his clothes to change into and he took her place in the bathroom. The days before, you could have cut the tension in the air with a knife. The tension had been all possibility. Now, the knife would stick mid-air, snared in the dense tangle of unsaid words, and their weight was the threat of things breaking down.

"I don't want to go back," Delphine said when they were both clean, and dressed, and weighed down by not saying. She glanced at Hardwick quickly, watching his face for signs of pain, and added: "I know it sounds awful..."

"Plenty of people prefer not to spend Christmas with their family."

"Like you?" Her lips curved into a smile that was a ghost of the one she'd gifted him earlier. "I don't have your excuse."

Hardwick shrugged. "If my parents were still around, I'd spend the holiday with them."

"I'm sorry." Delphine covered her eyes. "I didn't even think—"

"It's okay. I didn't mean that as an attack. Just..." He shrugged again. "It was easier having other people around who had the same issue as I did. Sensing lies didn't hurt them like it hurts me, but it still gave them a weird feeling. Telling the truth came naturally to us."

Delphine lowered her hands. Her gaze was distant. "I imagine it would be easier," she said, and the note of longing in her voice made his heart twist. "My father died when I was ten. Maybe if he—but that doesn't matter. It's just my mother and my two younger brothers now. And the rest of the extended family."

"Jackson said a shifter family had booked out half the town."

"Only half?" Delphine reached for her drink. "It was all right last year. I was here for work, and Mum and the boys came over to surprise me. There was enough for them to do that I could stay out of the spotlight, but with everyone here..." Her fingers fidgeted on the glass. "You'd think it'd be easier to blend in in a crowd. But my family is so into... family things."

"Like everyone being a shifter."

She nodded and picked up her glass at last. "Like everyone being a shifter," she echoed, and sipped.

"How have you managed to keep the truth hidden so long?"

She met his eyes and tapped her temple, one eyebrow raised.

"By lying. Right. I want to know the specifics."

Delphine let out a deep breath. "The specifics... okay."

She sounded relieved. Hardwick knew why. This wasn't the question she'd been dreading. The one whose answer she kept locked up so deep inside it was like sitting next to a construction site.

"How do you know if someone's a shifter? One, they shift in front of you. That's a fairly solid giveaway. But it's not the only way. Two, if they're a shifter and you are too, you can speak telepathically. Which is easy to get through in a big group setting, where everyone might has well be talking at once and even if they aren't, you can pretend to be so focused on whatever you're doing, or another conversation, or one of the kids trying to fly up the chimney to find Santa that you always have an excuse for not catching on. And—" She grimaced. "It helps when you know they're only going to be talking about certain things, anyway. The pool of conversation at most of my family gatherings in not particularly deep."

"You just fake it. How long have you been doing this?"

"Three. When you look deep into a shifter's eyes, you can sometimes catch a glimpse of their inner animal. Especially if said inner animal is having strong feelings about whatever's happening, like the roast's just come out of the oven, or someone has impugned the family honor by not rolling over and letting grandmother use them as a bridge over a muddy puddle, or whatever other horrific slight she can come up with. Solution: don't look at them. That one's easy."

"Delphine, that's horrible."

"As for your question..." She seemed to wrestle with it. "Fifteen years?"

The bottom dropped out of Hardwick's stomach. No wonder just being in her presence made his head hurt. "Why?"

"That's the question, isn't it."

She scooped up a forkful of lasagna, avoiding his eyes.

"I can't," she said at last. "I can't tell you."

"You can tell me anything."

"It's not just about me. There's someone else who—" She shook her head firmly. "I need this to keep working. It's—important. It might be *horrible*, and hard, but it's working."

To his horror, his head remained clear. She was telling the truth; whatever she was trying to achieve, lying to her entire family was letting her do it.

"It's working," she repeated, quietly, "And it—it doesn't matter, anyway, because you're not going to meet them."

"What are you talking about?"

She looked at him then, her expression determined. "You're not going to meet my family."

"But I'm your mate."

The words were awkward on his tongue. As he watched Delphine's face close over, he realized that was the first time either of them had said it out loud.

He'd just claimed her out loud as his mate, in the same breath as he was telling her what to do.

"And you're a griffin shifter who feels lies like someone's beating you up." Her mouth twitched. "If I'm around my family—if we're together when I'm with them—I don't want to hurt you."

"You could tell them the truth."

She stared. "That isn't an option."

"Why not?"

"Is this an interrogation?"

Sitting there on the other side of the table, she'd never seemed more distant. It was worse than before they'd touched. Before she'd shuddered beneath him, soft and delicate against his rough-hewn edges, but so full of longing it was as though she didn't notice how delicate she was. The way she'd strained against him, wanting more of *him*, his touch and his roughness, and brought out a roughness in him he hadn't known existed.

She'd made herself vulnerable to him. Taken that open heart he'd laid out for her and opened hers in exchange. And they were right back where they started.

Only worse, because now he was acting like that moment of vulnerability meant he got to tell her what to do.

"Delphine, I—"

"I said I don't want to hurt you." She stabbed her fork into a bite of lasagna, then put it down. Stood up, her eyes burning into his. "Don't hurt me in return."

She grabbed her plate and stalked round-shouldered into the bedroom.

Hardwick groaned.

*That could have gone better*, he thought.

His griffin shrugged its wings. He sighed, propping his head on one hand.

It was right.

Could have gone better? Really? For either of them, given who they were?

Later that night, he knocked on the bedroom door.

"Delphine?"

She wasn't asleep. When he opened the door, she sat up against the bed's headboard and tipped her head back. Her honey-colored eyes shone in the light from his side of the door.

"I shouldn't have said any of that," he said. "I told myself I'd let you be. Before, when I hadn't told you that I was your mate. Being your mate doesn't give me the right to tell you what to do."

"Doesn't give me the right not to be judged by you for it, either." She gave a weak smile.

"I can't judge you. I don't know what you've been through."

"And I won't tell you." Her smile became a grimace. "I guess we're at an impasse. And it doesn't matter anyway, does it? If we're stuck here?"

He gazed at her. At the hope in her eyes.

"No," he said. "Not if we're stuck here."

"Spend the night with me?"

He lay down on the bed beside her, holding her close and thanking the stars that she couldn't sense the turmoil in his heart.

Tomorrow was Christmas Eve. The blizzard showed no signs of blowing itself out. For the next few days, it was just going to be the two of them, together.

Maybe that would be time enough for one of them to back down.

His griffin shook its wings and he sighed.

*You're right*, he told it. *Maybe that'll be time enough for me to back down.*

He hadn't lied to her. He wouldn't tell her what to do or force her to let him meet her family if she didn't want that.

But she was still unhappy. And everything he was wanted to save her from that.

# 19

# DELPHINE

She had a plan. She could stay with Hardwick, out here, by themselves, and they could find their way together through the strange, magical, discomforting thing between them. Without the person she was in the outside world interfering.

That was the plan. Then, on their third day together—Christmas Eve—the roof came down.

The creaking had grown louder all night. In the morning, before she was awake enough to remember the difference between what she wanted to do and what she told herself she should be doing, Delphine made her way to the kitchen to stoke the stove and put on the kettle for more terrible coffee.

*Scones,* she thought absently, then *after caffeine. Even if it is terrible caffeine.*

She knew herself well enough to know that she was in the sort of mood where one spilled spoonful of flour or dropped piece of butter would send her into childish tears. It wasn't just the lack of sleep. It was something under her skin. Restless, unhappy energy. Ready to snap.

Nothing had ever gotten to her like this before. Not her boss's blindness to the fact that he'd employed a non-shifter. Not the way she'd become so successful at blending into the background at her own family events that these days, nobody even asked if she wanted to join them on the wing. Not even her family's snide remarks about her mother.

She couldn't let herself explode now. The thought of Hardwick seeing her lose it—

*Hardwick.* Her surly, exhausted rescuer, whose life she'd completely interrupted and who treated her like she was a bomb about to go off, and yet who already felt like someone she had known all her life.

Her mate.

Her *soulmate.*

It must be because he had figured out her secret, she thought. Her chest thudded strangely, and the roof groaned as though in sympathy. He knew her secret, but she hadn't had to *say* anything. It was… it was almost as good as telling the truth.

Wasn't it?

In the next room, the bed creaked as Hardwick rolled over. "Delphine—" he muttered. His voice was still rough with sleep.

She bit back a moan. Did he have to say her name like… like that? Like he was having some sort of incredible dream?

Why the hell had she gotten out of bed again?

She cleared her throat. "Hardwick? Are you feeling up to some coffee?"

"Delphine." The sleepy roughness was gone now. He sat up, though, which provided new distractions: his sleep-ruffled hair. His face creased from the pillow. A slow blink, his expression vague and muddled, just for a moment, before the usual lines deepened around his mouth and eyes. "Do you hear that?"

"Hear what?"

The roof groaned again just as she said it, like it was trying to prove her a liar. She frowned. "It's just the house settling, isn't it? All that snow—"

The groaning crescendoed into a tearing sound. Hardwick leapt to his feet.

"Watch out!" he shouted, and before Delphine had time to wonder what she was watching out for, everything went white.

*Really?* Delphine thought. *Twice in one week?*

Which answered the question of whether she was alive. Answered it before she'd thought of asking it, even. Which left… how?

It took her a moment to remember that she had a body full of nerve endings she could use to figure that out. The shock of the crash felt like it had dislocated her mind. Bit by bit, she crept back into herself.

"Ow," she muttered.

Her mind itched.

"Hardwick?" she gasped. Now that her nerve endings were back online, she could tell she was on her back on the floor, covered with what felt like a heavy blanket. Or possibly the sofa. How the hell had the sofa gotten on top of her?

Her left leg was cold. So was her right arm. She curled her fingers and felt snow crunch between them. Snow? Really? *Inside?*

What *happened?*

And why was the sofa moving?

Her other hand squeezed into the tight gap between herself and the heavy lump and she realized with another thud that it wasn't furniture on top of her. It was Hardwick, in his griffin form. He was crouched over her, his griffin body protecting her from whatever had just happened.

The noise. The snow. Holy hell, had the roof caved in?

Her fingers brushed against Hardwick's... chest? Feathers, soft beneath her fingertips, transitioning to rough fur lower down.

"Are you all right?" she asked.

Her mind itched again. She gnawed on the inside of her cheek, frustrated. "Of course. I can't hear you.

I'm—I'm not hurt." She was pretty sure that was the truth. "If you're going to try to move, talk to me. I can feel it, like an itch. If you're not going to move—"

*If you can't move.* Her mouth went dry. If he was injured…

"If you're not going to move, don't say anything, and I'll know that's what you're trying to tell me."

Her mind itched.

Oh, thank God.

Hardwick stood up slowly. His huge chest heaved as he pushed himself off the ground, and his claws dug into the wooden floorboards. Something creaked above him. He was supporting what looked like half the roof on his back.

He flicked his beak towards what a few moments ago had been the door. Delphine got the message at once. She shuffled on her elbows in the small space he'd created for her and scrambled free.

Seconds later, Hardwick surged after her, shedding snow and broken beams.

She got to her feet and gaped.

The cabin looked as though a meteor had struck it. The roof was almost completely caved in. All that was left was most of one wall on one side and the remains of the solid old stove in the middle.

The wind bit at her bare arms. She was still wearing the clothes she'd gone to bed in, Hardwick's long-sleeved shirt and a pair of his boxers.

He took one look at her, his eagle eyes sharp, and dug around in the ruins with his foreclaws. She caught his heavy winter coat when he threw it at her and pulled it on, then poked around and found her own boots while he hunted out clothes for himself.

At least she'd left her boots at the front door. They were easy to find. Squashed, but easy to find.

She pulled them on, ran her hands through her hair and shook out the bits of snow and splinters they dislodged, and muttered: "Well, *shit*."

Hardwick gave her a look that suggested the same sentiment was going through his mind. He tossed snow on the ruins of the stove, quenching the last of the fire.

She gave him privacy while he shifted and dressed and leaned into his embrace when he wrapped his arms around her.

"I guess this is it," he murmured.

Delphine pulled the heavy coat more closely around herself and turned around so they were facing each other. She pressed her face into the crook of his neck and sighed.

"We're heading back to Pine Valley."

# 20

# HARDWICK

He'd half expected Delphine to drag her heels, but she was surprisingly efficient.

She checked the power situation and turned off the electricity so they weren't risking the house burning down after they left – or what was left of it burning down, anyway. She checked the rubble for a duffel bag and stashed all the extra clothes he managed to dig out into it.

This was a side to her he hadn't seen, he realized, as he watched her close her eyes and take a slow, deep breath. Her shoulders straightened, her spine uncurled, but somehow she didn't seem any bigger.

Delphine caught him looking at her and grimaced. "Sorry," she said. "It's just, if we're going back… I want to be ready."

He looked at her again and understanding struck. When her shoulders and back were curved in, she was drawing attention to herself. By straightening up, she made herself more neutral. Her pose, her expression, the way she moved—it was all designed to let her slip through the world unnoticed.

"What?" Delphine asked, and he explained his theory. Her lips twitched. "Well, it's a good thing none of my family are as observant as you are. Come on. Let's… get this over with."

They would go to the car first, they decided. Part of Delphine's new careful neutrality was making sure she arrived back in Pine Valley with the bottles of port she'd left it to buy.

The bottles were frozen solid. One of them had burst, and Delphine looked at it for longer than Hardwick was comfortable with before closing the trunk on it. When she caught him staring at her, his massive griffin's head tipped to one side, she explained with an uncomfortable smile, "I wondered if it might be useful, somehow, still, even though it's broken. I don't think so, though."

She rolled the intact bottles in spare clothing and secured them in the duffel bag.

He held the duffel in one foreclaw and knelt down so she could climb onto his back. She was more confident this time.

He wasn't. The one good thing about her plan to drive into town by herself, he'd reckoned, was that it meant less time when he was terrified out of his mind thinking he was going to drop her. Now? He had to fly close enough to town that they could walk the rest of the way, while keeping out of sight of anyone else taking advantage of the good weather to explore the snow. It was a job for agility and speed, sharp turns to take cover in the trees or drop to the ground and camouflage himself among the rocks. Not a job for keeping his mate in one piece.

He gingerly took to the air.

They would go to the Heartwells. That was the plan. Hardwick hadn't met them, but after he explained to Delphine where exactly she'd crashed the car in relation to the town, she'd decided the Heartwells' home was closer than Jackson's place. They could bypass the town entirely and only be in danger of being seen by the most intrepid Christmas Eve cross-country skiers.

The Heartwells' lodge. Hardwick had never seen it, but Delphine's instructions had been clear enough. Farther up than the town, in another of the steep, snow-filled valleys that these mountains were full of.

She was sure the dragon shifters would help. Hardwick was less sure, but at least they'd be among shifters, on the shifters' home turf. He wouldn't have to worry about the background ache of being around people who were constantly, whether they realized it or not, lying about their true natures.

Not around people, anyway. Person. Delphine was still—

*!!!*

What was that?

His griffin flared its wings in surprise. Delphine squeaked and tightened her grip on his feathers.

"What is it?" she asked as he hovered in place.

He didn't know. Even if he could talk to her, he wouldn't have anything to say.

Hardwick reached for the glowing mate bond, trying again to send something, anything through it. Reassurance? Calm? Again, the light slipped through his fingers.

*!!!*

It wasn't a noise. It felt like telepathy, except it wasn't words. Hardwick banked his wings, coasting over the snow-covered tips of the trees as his griffin raked the landscape for any sign of what could have made the not-sound.

They were still out of sight of the town and the lodge. The mountain landscape here looked untouched: smooth snow lay like a comforter over dark tumbles of rock and sky-piercing pine trees. Hardwick knew better than to believe that. Hell, the town was called *Pine Valley*. It had probably been a forestry outpost before the local industry had switched over to tourism. Mining, too, maybe. That picture-perfect snow probably hid abandoned mineshafts, rusted tools—any number of dangers.

A ridge pushed up towards the sky ahead of them. The lodge should be visible from the other side; he could see the cut in the trees where the road wove its way to the lowest part of it, a gentle dip that didn't deserve the name 'saddle.' Careful to keep far enough from the road that no one driving on it could see him, Hardwick swooped around, preparing to climb over the—

*Fire! Come on, flames! Go!*

He would have liked to say he was prepared that time. Instead, his griffin almost jumped out of the air.

"Hardwick!" Delphine yelped. She boosted herself closer to his head, arms wrapped around his neck. "Is everything all right?"

Hardwick swung his head from side to side, searching. He still couldn't see anything, but he could definitely hear it.

Someone was out there. Some... kid?

The voice didn't sound like an adult. Hardwick frowned. He looked for a clear patch of rock and landed.

Delphine slipped from his back. "What's the matter? The Heartwells should be just over that ridge."

He waved one wing at her and concentrated on shifting. She turned away as he transformed—then turned back, hesitantly. Her cheeks were already red from the cold, but he imagined they would have gotten red then, anyway.

"About that whole shifting-with-your-clothes thing—" she began.

He cocked one eyebrow at her. "You're not enjoying the view?"

She didn't need to answer; the sparkle in her eye and the tilt of her chin as she made a show of looking away were answer enough. Then she went serious. "I told you my family take that sort of thing seriously. I still think we should do whatever we can to not force a meeting, but..." She sighed and shook her head.

*She's ashamed of me.* The thought had legs.

Delphine wrapped her arms around herself. "Don't get me wrong. No one would say anything to your face. But they'd say it in a way that hurt." She stretched out one hand to brush against his forehead.

She wasn't ashamed of him. She was concerned.

"Emotionally or because of my power?"

"A true Belgrave would never limit themselves to just one," she replied acerbically.

"Sounds like a lot of chest-thumping bullshit." He pulled on his pants and jacket.

"Don't be ridiculous. Belgraves would never be so crass as to thump their chests."

Hardwick finished fastening his jacket and turned to her. "Delphine, you know I don't care what other people think of me, right?"

She bit her lip and looked away.

Right. *She* cared.

Hardwick pushed away a sudden prickle of unease. *Was* she ashamed of him? Was she—no. He shook his head.

"I landed because I thought I heard something."

"I didn't hear anything."

"Telepathically."

Delphine almost managed to hide her wince. "Oh."

He wrapped one arm around her. "I didn't mean it like that."

"I know." She leaned her forehead against his shoulder. "I just... need to get my head back in the game. I can't slip up like that once I'm back around my family."

Hardwick kissed her gently on the top of her head, frowning. He'd hoped, after last night, that she would start to rethink the need to lie to her people. Apparently not.

"Anyway. What did you hear?"

"At first, it sounded like..." He gestured, trying to put words to it. "Not words. More like when you hear something loud, and it echoes in your ears. But just the echo, not the noise."

"Like someone screaming?"

"I don't know. And then—"

*Screw you, snow! Screw you, stupid mountain! Stupid Christmas! Stupid flames!*

"—Sounds like a kid," he said, and told her what he'd just heard.

She looked concerned. "Are they in trouble?"

"I think so."

"Can you tell where they are?"

"Not from here. And not from just their telepathy. It's not directional, like hearing someone shout out loud. Hard to trace back to the source."

"You don't have to explain that to me." Delphine pulled away.

He raised his eyebrows. "Thought you might find it helpful. You don't need to guess what's going on if I'm that guy who narrates his own every action."

"...Oh." She leaned against him again. "Thanks. I'm sorry for being so suspicious."

"This is new for you, same as it is for me."

"I never thought about what it would mean, having someone who knew my secret. I never planned—" She looked as though she was about to say more, then shook her head. "Forget about me. What about this kid? How can we find him to check on him?"

"Easy."

She stared at him, waiting for him to continue, and then swore. "For goodness' sake. Did I hit my head? You heard him using telepathy, you can respond to him just the same." She paused. "You could have while we were still in the air."

"I wanted to keep you in the loop."

Again, she looked surprised. Hardwick filed that away in a folder labelled *fucking Belgraves* and squeezed her hand.

*Hello!* he called, sending his telepathic voice as wide as he could. *Can you hear me? Do you need help?*

There was a pause. Then: *No-o! I don't need any help!*

Pain shot through Hardwick's head. He hissed and bit back a curse.

Delphine pulled off one glove and put her hand on his forehead. "Let me guess. Whoever it is, they're completely fine?"

"Got it in one," he gritted out.

She rubbed one thumb over his temple. He leaned into her caress.

"Bet he doesn't want his parents to know he's in trouble out here, either."

"Good point." Hardwick laced his fingers through hers so her hand wouldn't get cold. "One sec."

*Hey, sure. You don't need any help. Maybe you could help me. I'm trying to find the Heartwell lodge—*

*Don't tell them I'm here!*

*Buddy, I don't even know where 'here' is. What are you doing?*

*I'm not lost!*

Hardwick grimaced. "Ow."

Delphine squeezed his hand silently and he added: "He says he's not lost."

"You don't say. You know, this is all sounding really familiar. Stuck out in the snow, trying to convince yourself everything's fine, you can totally handle it…" She stared up at him, her honey-colored eyes worried. "I know he's a shifter, whoever he is, but we can't just leave him out here."

"I know." He scanned the mountainside around them. *My name's Hardwick Jameson. I'm on vacation here, seeing a friend of mine. Jackson Gilles. Do you know him?*

*You know Mr. Gilles? That—doesn't matter! 'Cos nothing's wrong. I—argh!*

Hardwick was still wincing from the 'nothing's wrong' when the kid's voice suddenly cut out. Delphine tugged on his arm.

"There!" She pointed at a patch of snow further along the ridge. "That collapsed just as you got hurt."

"Let's go."

They hurried up the slope. The snow here was deep, but there were enough rocky outcrops that they could scramble up to where the snow had collapsed without getting too deep. Hardwick kept a careful eye on Delphine. Her lips were pale and pinched, but she was refusing to say anything was wrong, even though he knew she must be comparing this to what had happened to her.

He kept talking to the kid the whole way. The kid responded mostly in groans and complaints that this was so embarrassing, and they should just leave him here to die. Hardwick took that as a good sign.

The snow crumbled a bit more as they reached it, as though something was disturbing it from underneath. Hardwick pulled his jacket off. "I'll shift and start digging," he said.

Delphine took his clothes and knelt down. "Can you hear me?" she called. There was a muffled screech in reply, and she went pale. "Cole? Is that you?"

Another screech… this one definitely closer to the 'embarrassed' side of the equation than the 'in mortal peril' side.

Hardwick dug into the snow with his foreclaws. They weren't well designed for scratching at snow, but he managed to haul the slip away within a few minutes. He stayed in constant communication with the kid, and when they figured he was getting close, he eased off on digging.

*How you going in there?*

*I can see something—wait! Hah!*

Hardwick lurched backwards just in time to avoid a plume of red flame bursting from the hole. Delphine yelled in surprise, then darted forward before he could stop her.

"Cole!" she cried out. "What are you doing in there?"

A small dragon slithered out of the hole. The snow it had melted glittered on its black scales, then exploded through the air like droplet diamonds as it shook itself. The dragonling—Cole?—was the size of a small pony, but long and skinny, like someone had taped limbs to a big snake. It checked over its scales and sent little puffs of flame to melt the snow still clinging them.

*Sorry, Miss Belgrave,* he said, curling himself into a sad pretzel.

Delphine crossed her arms. She gave no sign that she hadn't heard him.

Hardwick decided to step in. He shifted and dressed quickly, frustrated by the delay of having to pull on clothes. Delphine was right, he should figure out whatever trick the other shifters had found to bring their clothes with them when they shifted. Not for chest-thumping reasons, but for practicality. Frostbite took longer to set in for shifters than it did for regular humans, but it did set in eventually. And cold was cold, regardless of whether your veins were actually closing up or not.

"How'd you end up out here, kid?" he asked once he was safely human-shaped and dressed.

The dragon's tail whipped. *I'm not telling!*

Delphine raised her eyebrows at Hardwick. "I think the real question is how *long* he's been out here."

*Umm...*

Hardwick groaned. "That's the sort of non-answer that tells the whole story," he said for Delphine's benefit.

*It's not my fault! I had to get it done before Christmas!* The dragonling stared beseechingly at Delphine..

And said something to her that Hardwick couldn't hear.

Damn.

Well, if he couldn't translate for her, he could at least distract. He touched her arm. "We should keep moving. I don't know about you two, but I'd rather keep talking somewhere with a roof over my head and something to eat, rather than out here."

"Good thinking. Cole, we were heading up to your place and hoping to borrow a car to get back into town. Want to come with us? We could knock on the front door while you sneak in round the back. Not that you're here because you snuck out, or anything."

*Yeah, maybe, but... oh, no. Too late.*

Cole looked like he wanted to jump back down his hole. Hardwick followed his gaze, shading his eyes against the sunlight, and Delphine followed suit a moment later. If you didn't know she hadn't heard half the conversation, you never would have guessed she was making it up on the fly.

It made him feel uneasy. The whole thing did. Even playing along with her. It wasn't lying, but it was close enough that he could feel the ghost of a knife behind his temples, waiting to stab down.

"Oh..." Delphine breathed, and he guessed as she hesitated that she'd been about to say 'no'. "...good. The whole family's here."

Winged figures were appearing over the distant ridge. They were sinuous, glittering creatures that soared through the air like fish through water.

Cole sank to the ground, groaning pitifully.

"Don't worry," Delphine told him. "I'm sure they'll just be pleased to see you—oh."

More figures appeared behind the dragons. These ones didn't fly like elegant sea-creatures. Their wings pummeled the air like it had insulted their mothers. They were stocky and powerful, similar to and yet so different from what Hardwick remembered of seeing his parents flying.

Not griffins. Winged lions.

Delphine's family.

"What are they doing here?" she said under her breath.

Hardwick stepped closer to her. "Maybe they were looking for you, after all," he murmured.

"No." Delphine shaded her eyes and peered up into the sky. "No, that can't be—oh, blast. Just call them, will you? I'll say I was busy with Cole."

Hardwick hailed the distant shifters, but they had already spotted them anyway. The dragons curved towards them and the nearest, which was the color of mother of pearl, sent a message directly to Hardwick's mind.

*Cole's down there with you? He's been gone all night!*

"You've been gone all night?" Hardwick echoed. Cole wriggled miserably.

*Only ONE night! And the weather was looking better yesterday! And anyway, I'm fourteen! I can look after myself!*

Hardwick's head hurt. He couldn't tell whether it was because of lies, or because of teenagers.

*Both,* he thought gloomily.

"At least you found cover," Delphine said. Her voice was cheerful, but she was watching the winged lions with an uncertain look in her eyes. "Lucky you found the cave."

How was she managing it, Hardwick thought, amazed. Carrying on her own half of the conversation as though she could hear the other half. He was helping, but she was picking up his hints and running with them.

It couldn't always be like this, he realized. Most of the time she must be running blind, with no one to provide translation for her. What would that mean?

She must come off as absent-minded as best. Uncaring at worst. She would talk over other people, ignore their questions, seem like she was more interested in the sound of her own voice than anyone else's opinions.

And *that* was the lie she'd happily built her life around?

Delphine wasn't arrogant, or unfeeling. She was observant, and kind. He'd seen that over the last few days. Even when she'd doubted her own feelings. Even when she'd figured out he was hiding the truth of their connection from her. She'd gotten to the bottom of *his* problem, *his* hurt, before trying to get anything for herself—even the truth.

Hardwick barely noticed the three full-grown dragons that landed in a semi-circle around the two of them. His attention was all on the winged lion shifters that thudded to the ground further uphill.

They were solid, stocky creatures. Like tanks with wings, he thought. Golden-haired as Delphine, with wings ranging from pure white to gold-speckled and autumn-toned. Her family.

The people she was so afraid of knowing the truth, she'd twisted her whole life around lying to them.

His griffin's hackles rose.

What had they done, to make her think that was the only way she could live?

# 21

# DELPHINE

U ncle Martin. Aunt Grizelda. Several cousins: Brutus, Livia, and Pebbles. And her own brothers, wirier than the others, but still close enough to the classic Belgrave template that they'd never had any trouble fitting in.

Delphine resisted the urge to move closer to Hardwick. Except—was that the right thing to do? If he was her mate, and everyone was surely about to find out that particular fact, then maybe it would be natural for her to move closer to him. But how? Casually? Territorially?

She tried to remember how some of her cousins had acted when they brought their mates to family vacations for the first time. Pebbles had met her mate, a stunning bird of paradise, three years before. She had brought him home for Christmas that year. Delphine had spent most of the holiday in the kitchen, but she remembered how Pebbles had shown Pascal off. She'd practically glowed with happiness, preening and sticking to Pascal's side as though she couldn't bear to be apart from him. And even though a bird of paradise wasn't exactly the sort of shifter the olds had expected to match with a Belgrave, she'd been so *proud* of him.

Delphine was proud of Hardwick, too. Wasn't she? He was a *griffin*, for God's sake. No one could complain about that.

But no matter how hard she tried to pull on a mask of satisfied pride and smugness, what she really was, was terrified. Terrified that this was the moment that everything she'd worked so hard for was about to collapse. Terrified that her family would know what she really was.

Terrified that she was going to hurt Hardwick, badly.

Terrified that the deeper truth they had both been avoiding was not that they were mates, but that they were impossible. That she'd spent most of her life painstakingly transforming herself into something that was so opposite to what Hardwick needed that they could never be together.

Her chest tightened. No, that can't be possible. There had to be a way out, a way to fix this, a way to make everything okay again.

Something itched against the back of her mind. Just what she needed: someone trying to speak to her telepathically. Which had been fine when it was Cole—it wasn't hard to guess what teenaged boy who'd been snowed into his secret bunker overnight would try to say to get himself out of trouble, and even if the distracted–older–family–friend act hadn't worked, Hardwick had been amazing, translating for her.

She didn't even know who was trying to speak to her. It could have been anybody.

Delaying would only make things worse. She had to make a choice.

Delphine leaned against Hardwick and raised her eyebrows at Cole. "Too late to run now," she said. Cole hung his head and her mind itched again. She gave him a sympathetic smile, assuming that was what he was after, then took Hardwick's hand and looked up at him.

"Too late for us, too," she said. "Are you ready to meet my family?"

"Are you?" he replied in an undertone.

She kept her smile fixed on her face. "I don't think I should answer that."

A shadow passed across Hardwick's face and for a moment she was worried her smile would slip. She squeezed his hand and turned back to the crowd.

Goodness. Three full-grown dragons, and half a dozen winged lions. Her relatives must be *hating* this. Winged lions were around the size of regular lions; full-grown dragons were, frankly, *massive.*

Which gave her just the in she needed.

"Opal! Hank! Jasper!" she cried out, greeting the three dragons.

Opal and Hank were Cole's parents. Opal's scales were pale and luminescent, like her namesake, while Hank was a shade of forest green that would almost have counted as camouflage if it wasn't the middle of winter and he wasn't unmistakably dragon-shaped. Jasper, Opal's younger brother, was a thousand brilliant shades of red, orange and brown.

They all bent their heads to her in greeting, and the itch in her mind intensified. She waited for it to fade, then shaded her eyes against the light and added: "I don't think there's enough room out here for all of us in our animal forms! Shall I do introductions in human form, and then we can all head back somewhere warm?"

For another group of shifters, it might not have worked, but because both the Heartwells and her own family knew how to do Mr. Petrakis's trick with clothes, it did. Even cold-resistant shifters might not be too happy to hang out on a snowy mountainside stark naked, but the Belgraves leapt at the chance to show off their new skills—and to be, in human size, not completely physically outmatched by the dragon shifters.

Hardwick rubbed his thumb over the back of her hand, and she realized she was holding onto him with a death grip. She took a deep breath while the others were distracted by shifting and pulled herself together.

There were small rushes of air and sparks all around as the dragons and winged lions shifted back into human form.

The Heartwell siblings, Jasper and Opal, were both tall and broad-shouldered, with red hair and sparkling eyes the colors of the gems they were named after. Hank, who had married into the family and taken Opal's name, was a giant of a man with brown hair and eyes the same color as his dragon's scales. Jasper was dressed up as brightly as his dragon, in a hideous Christmas sweater and matching boots and hat that clashed incredibly with his red hair. Opal and Hank were slightly more normally dressed, though Delphine noticed a giveaway embroidered reindeer under the open collar of Opal's long jacket.

Beside her, Cole sighed and transformed back into a lanky teenaged boy. His hair was darker than either of his parents', and he'd shot up at least a foot since Delphine had last seen him. He was also, to his bad luck, wearing pajamas. Opal tsked and advanced on him threateningly, already pulling off her own coat to wrap around him. "Mom, no!" he cried, backing away.

She left them to it and turned to her own family.

Her heart did its usual complicated thing, because as terrified as she was at the idea of her family finding out the truth about her, she *did* love them. And this group weren't the most terrifying. Her grandparents weren't there, of course—she guessed that, if they'd all set out from the Heartwell lodge to find Cole, Grandmother would be waiting there, taking the opportunity to privately sneer at the dragon shifters' base. Uncle Carrick wasn't there, either. A little of the weight came off her chest.

Delphine's brothers, Vance and Anders, were identical twins. Like all Belgrave men they were tall with golden hair, and at almost-eighteen they were just starting the transformation from teenaged weed to burly full-grown adult.

They went through phases of wanting to look exactly like each other or not like each other at all. This was their first year at university. Early, of course; they were Belgraves, after all. Vance had gone to university in England and Anders had taken a year in the Netherlands, and they'd returned home at midterm to discover that they'd both changed up their look in exactly the same way. Long hair in a ponytail, truly terrible little moustache. In a huff, they'd both immediately gone and shaved off said moustache and lopped off the ponytail—then come back and huffed again.

Ponytail and moustache were back now, of course. They'd gotten over their annoyance at discovering how similar they were, *again*, and had cultivated the horrible hair in preparation for the extended family Christmas.

The others all shifted, too, and clambered through the snow to get closer now that there weren't three massive dragons in the way. Pebbles was a few years older than her, and even more blinged out than usual—Delphine suspected Pascal's influence, and of course being able to shift with jewelry as well as clothes would help unruffle any grandparents' feathers about her mate. Colored stones glittered on her fingers and in rows up her ears.

Pebbles' parents, Uncle Martin and Aunt Grizelda, were the same as ever: muscular and distant. Brutus, who if Delphine remembered correctly, had just turned twenty-one, was sporting a new undercut, and Livia, fourteen, looked as though she was trying not to look puffed from the recent flight. She had only had her First Flight the year before and was probably still getting used to her wings.

"Hello, you lot," she said cheerfully, waving them over. "How are you all liking Pine Valley so far?"

"That's it?" Anders said, feigning outrage. "That's all you've got to say for yourself after going missing? We've been out night and day—"

"Wearing ourselves to the bone with worry," Vance interjected.

"—not eating, not sleeping, worried sick—"

"Give it a rest." Delphine waited for Anders to get close enough, then aimed a half-hearted smack at the side of his head. He ducked out of the way, his outrage reaching pantomime levels. Vance, cunningly, was staying just out of reach. "You didn't really come look for me, did you?"

The twins glanced at one another, so quickly she almost missed it. "Course not," Anders said. Hardwick cleared his throat. "We joined the search for the dragonling when Mr. Heartwell said he'd gone missing."

"Mum's not with you?"

"Nah. She's doing a you, holing up with the olds so the rest of us can relax a bit. Speaking of..."

Both twins' eyes flicked to Hardwick and back to her.

"Not that we're prying—"

"We're not even asking, we're that good—"

"But if we were—"

"On the off-chance..."

Anders dropped to his knees. "Please tell us you managed to find some of Grandad's bloody plonk."

"Right. *That's* the question you wanted to ask." Delphine crossed her arms.

"It's been three days, Delphy! It's *life or death*." Anders collapsed entirely and rolled onto his back. "And *death* is more attractive by the minute. I can't believe the Grandad we've known all these years was happy drunk Grandad."

That was a scary thought.

"And Grandma's even been asking about you," Vance added.

That was even scarier.

"I've been busy," Delphine said. "Don't worry, I didn't forget about the shopping." She hooked one finger around the duffel bag at Hardwick's feet and lifted it so the bottles clinked. Anders gave a dramatic sigh of relief.

"Delphine!" Aunt Grizelda called out to her. "Aren't you going to introduce us?"

Vance grumbled, almost but not quite under his breath, "Oh, ruin it why don't you. I was trying to find a way to make 'I've been busy' dirty."

"You're stuck on *that*?" Anders exclaimed. "Are you even my brother? Come on. It's a classic. She didn't come back 'cos she was getting *biz*—"

"Aunt Grizelda, Uncle Martin." Delphine strenuously ignored her brothers. "I'd like to introduce you to Hardwick Jameson." The way she was squeezing his hand should have given the game away, but she said it anyway: "I should probably tell Mother or Grandfather and Grandmother first, but... Hardwick is my mate."

Aunt Grizelda gave a smile that almost made it to the corners of her lips. "Hardwick, was it? And you are…?"

Hardwick held her gaze and her smile didn't move an inch.

"How nice," she said.

Hardwick's eyelid flickered.

*Ouch,* Delphine thought in sympathy. *This is not going to go well.*

She grabbed the duffel bag of clothes and bottles in a way that clearly indicated it would need human hands looking after it in transit, and the motley group of shifters prepared to leave. Delphine was about to get on Hardwick's back again when her pocket buzzed. She fumbled out her phone and stared at it, amazed.

If she'd had to guess who might be calling her, her boss would be top of the list. His retreat had been due to finish that day, and he probably had a thousand problems for her to solve on his way to the airport.

But it wasn't him. It was her mother.

Delphine felt strange as she scrolled through message after message from her mum. None of them were outright panicking, but just the fact that there were so many told her how worried she'd been.

Her mother. Worried about *her.*

Even though she was a Belgrave. Even though their family creed meant everyone should have thought she couldn't possibly be in any trouble.

That strange feeling still churning in her stomach, Delphine send a quick, reassuring message.

*I'm fine! Bumped into dragon search and rescue team on the way back. Poor Cole safe but going to be in trouble I think! See you soon!*

She got a response straight away.

*Thank God. Don't worry me like that again!*

Don't worry her? What was to worry about? As far as her mother was concerned...

Delphine shoved her phone back in her pocket and bit her lip.

As far as her mother knew, she had no reason to be worried. But if Hardwick meeting the rest of her family went as badly as she expected it to, then that would change.

# 22

# HARDWICK

The Belgraves were staying at the main hotel in town. Which was a small hotel, but the only one Pine Valley had. They'd booked out almost the entire place and, Hardwick discovered when they got there, had bullied the manager into giving them private access to the dining room for all their meals. Where the other guests went to eat, he didn't know, but he didn't blame them for not sticking around.

He wished the Heartwells had invited them for dinner. They had seemed like nice people.

Not that all the Belgraves rubbed him up the wrong way. Delphine's brothers were like any dickhead teens, more interested in their own lives than anyone else's, and her mother seemed nice. She was short and fine-boned, with faded blonde hair. Hardwick guessed she'd married into the family, and when he shook her hand, he got a glimpse of her inner animal: a housecat.

The Belgrave obsession with shifter status couldn't be that bad, he told himself.

Ten minutes into dinner, he was rethinking that assumption.

He was seated next to Delphine's aunt Grizelda, one of the shifters who'd been out looking for little Cole. He'd thought this was a good sign until she started talking.

"...The family used to be far stricter about it. But there are only so many winged lion shifter families in the world, after all!"

Hardwick frowned. "But the mate bond—"

"Oh, well, fate has always been a friend to the Belgraves. And really, it could be worse!"

*He* could be worse, she was saying. As though shifters existed on a sort of scale, with winged lions at the top and everyone else ranked below, griffins included.

Not just griffins, he realized as Grizelda kept talking.

"Take Pascal. Now, I'm not saying that dear Pebbles' mate isn't a *complete* darling, but, well, there's always the *risk*, isn't there? One minute the Belgraves are winged lion shifters, with a genealogy stretching back to before Minos exploded—you really *must* let me tell you about that one day, Hardwick darling, of course there's no written evidence but the *pictorial* is quite enough, and I've always felt such a *connection* with the islands—Well, what I'm saying is, their children might turn out a bit *colorful.*" She elbowed him, as though she'd just told a hilarious joke. "But as I said, fate has always been kind to us. The Belgrave winged lions *always* breed true."

Wow.

Hardwick was aware he was staring like a dead man. Worse, though, was the tension that whispered around the room. Not all the Belgraves shared in it. Pebbles—that couldn't be her real name, surely—leaned a little closer to her mate, Pascal, whose edges had gone all sharp. Delphine's mother went slightly pale, and Delphine...

...Was smiling, and laughing quietly at a joke someone else had told, and standing up to fetch another bottle of pinot gris for the table.

Hardwick's heart sank.

"Doesn't sound like a problem to me," he said. "Like you said, only so many lion shifters in the world, winged or not."

"*Exactly.*" Grizelda pursed her lips triumphantly and watched Delphine edge out of the room, arms full of empty bottles. "And like I said, we're not quite so strict anymore. Not since dear Delphy."

The door swung shut behind Delphine and the hairs on the back of Hardwick's neck prickled. "What about Delphine?"

Grizelda was all painted-on surprise. "Well! Her *mother*, of course. When we all heard that Dominic had—"

*CRASH!*

"Oh, shit!" One of the twins sprang up and started beating at his shirt, which was, somehow, on fire. "Come on, man, fire isn't fair play!"

"Neither's getting Livia to telepath you the answers, asshole!" The other one threw another candle at him and the first twin yelped and dodged out of the way. "Aren't you meant to be studying this shit?"

"Aren't you meant to be studying *med*, not setting fire to people?"

"*Boys.*"

The voice cut through the chaos. Both twins fell silent, and so did the rest of the table. Even Grizelda paused her story.

The man who had spoken was Delphine's grandfather, Alastair. He was seated at the head of the table and treated the position like a throne. His hair was pure silver, and his eyes a rusty gold that could control the whole room with a single look. His wife, Angela, was sitting next to him. Her hair was a paler silver and her eyes a darker bronze.

Delphine had introduced him to them both before the meal and they had waved him away. He didn't know whether to be insulted or relieved.

When conversation started to burble up again, he tried to steer the one he was having in a less disturbing direction.

"Must have been quite the undertaking, getting everyone out here. Pine Valley isn't exactly on the main route."

"Yes, it's quite off the beaten track! But after what dear Sara told us about last year—that's Delphine's mother but of *course* you know that already—we simply couldn't miss it. We all wondered what could have lured her away from a family Christmas, and now that we're here, we *quite* understand." Grizelda bared her teeth in a smile that had too many teeth in it to be truly friendly. "It's so *freeing*, don't you think, being so far away from human towns?"

"There are still humans in the town." Hardwick groaned internally. Did Jackson and the Heartwells know the Belgraves were being this slack about secrecy? "Anyway, I thought Delphine's family came here to see her last Christmas." Lured away, indeed.

"Oh, well." Grizelda waved away the idea of a mother wanting to see her daughter for Christmas rather than a horde of in-laws. "Delphy's adorable, of course. Such a sweetheart. But she's not exactly a team player, is she? Now, the twins—excellent value there. Why, when dear Brutus had his First Flight..."

Hardwick got the feeling his input wasn't needed for the rest of the conversation. He held his tongue for the next few minutes and was proved right. Grizelda was happy to hold forth indefinitely about her thoughts on the family, and when she eventually ran out of material, another Belgrave stepped in.

It was all the same rubbish. Belgrave this, Belgrave that, heritage this, unbroken line of shifters that. To hear them talk, there'd been a winged lion at every important event in European history for the last three thousand years. Hardwick was tempted to ask if there'd been a Belgrave ancestor propping up the manger.

Instead, he found his head was buzzing so badly he could only make out one word in ten. The haze of lies that covered the dinner table was circling him. They hit more like mallets than knives: dull, blunt trauma. Endless. Unstopping.

"Of course, we expected nothing less of our Livia—"

"And Brutus, you know, takes his studies so seriously—"

"*What* a surprise! Of course, I've always known that dear Delphy would do well…"

"—so *happy* for you both, *truly*—"

"Hardwick?"

Delphine. Her voice cut through the fog. Somewhere, a chair scraped. Hardwick fumbled for the golden light that connected her to him, but before he could get a grip on it, Delphine was beside him. He got a grip on her, instead.

Her hand was cool against his forehead. He could have told her there was no point. He wasn't sick, he was—

"We're going to head upstairs," she declared, her voice carrying in a way it hadn't ever before in front of her family. "It's been a long day—"

It hadn't. Not technically speaking. It had already been almost midday by the time the roof got them up. Hardwick cursed under his breath as pain shot through his skull, a vibrating crescendo above the haze.

Delphine's other hand tightened nervously on his shoulder.

"What's wrong with him, Delphy?" someone asked.

"Time for us to go." Delphine hooked his arm over her shoulder and helped him up. Hardwick silently thanked her for not even trying to answer whoever-it-was's question. She guided him to the door. Just before it shut behind them, Grizelda's voice rang out above the noise:

"A migraine, I suppose. Oh, it's a *human* thing, Papa. I wouldn't have thought shifters suffered from them, but, well. *You* know..."

With that heartening display of solidarity, Hardwick and Delphine stumbled into the foyer.

"I'm so sorry," Delphine said at once. Her voice was tight. "What do you need?"

"Silence."

She stiffened under his arm, and he swore at himself silently. "Not you. Them. Is there a room we can go to, or...?"

"Upstairs."

His head was still pounding. Delphine guided him through the foyer to the stairs, and he didn't make it easy for her. His feet wanted to give up and let him fall where he was standing. Eventually, however, they made it to the third floor and a small, tidy room that looked out over the street.

Delphine helped him onto the bed and fetched a glass of water. He drank it, gratefully, knowing he should be saying something but unable to form words.

"Hell," he managed at last. "Your Aunt Grizelda's a goddamn menace."

Delphine hiccup-laughed. "She's a level four," she said, and he must have looked either confused or about to pass out, because she added: "There are five levels. One is easy to deal with, five is hardest."

"Who's a five, then?"

"Grandfather and Grandmother." She stepped away again, and when she returned, she laid a cool, damp cloth on his forehead. "I can go, if you'd rather be on your own."

"No. God, Delphine. Stay here with me." *Away from them.*

She slipped into the bed, wrapping herself around him. Every movement made Hardwick's head throb, but he eased himself into a better position to put his arms around her. She lay her head against his shoulder, so close he could feel her heartbeat, and he tried to tell himself it made the pain less.

The ache in his head didn't agree.

"Is it better up here, or do we need to go somewhere else?" she asked.

Somewhere else. His mind went straight to the rustic cabin, and he groaned. That wasn't an option, even if sleeping in a pile of snow suddenly felt like the only thing that would stop his head from hurting. He turned the damp cloth on his forehead over and lay the cooler side over his eyes.

"Maybe a walk," Delphine suggested, "to get away from everyone."

Out on the streets wouldn't be an improvement. The town was full of happy families, happily lying their way through the holiday.

"Here's fine," he said. "I can't hear anyone. This place must have good sound insulation. If they have shifters staying here often, that's probably a good thing. Their guests would go mad, being able to hear every conversation in the building."

"Still... It's worse, isn't it?" she whispered. "Worse than you expected, I mean."

"Yeah."

She pressed her forehead against his shoulder. "Is there anything I can do?"

"Just stay here with me."

He curled one arm up to caress the back of her head. She made a soft, vulnerable noise and kissed his neck. He focused on that: her closeness, her gentleness, the warmth of her body against his.

Not the way part of the pain hazing his thoughts was because of her and had been ever since she saw her family appear in the sky.

"Hardwick—"

He flinched. He didn't mean to, but he'd let his guard down too much. She wasn't even lying. His body was reacting on automatic.

Delphine pushed herself up onto her elbows and looked down at him, her eyes shadowed.

"Delphine, I—"

"It's me, isn't it?"

He sighed. "I know you're not doing it on purpose."

"But I'm still doing it. I'm only laying here, and even though I'm with you, I'm still thinking: what if one of my relatives comes through that door?

What if they don't, but they still try to call out to me telepathically? Half my brain is constantly on the alert, working through ways to fix any possible situation, and... and it hurts you."

"It shouldn't." He couldn't bear the look in her eyes. He looked away. "Not if you don't lie out loud. I shouldn't react to you just thinking things."

"But you are." She sat up and swung her legs off the side of the bed. "You're meant to be detoxing."

"I'm—"

"You're sick. And me being here isn't helping."

Hardwick pushed himself upright. "It isn't your fault."

"But it is, isn't it? And even if it's not my fault, I can't stay here if I'm hurting you." She almost managed to hide the effort it took to keep herself together, and then something snapped, and she sagged. "Sorry. I shouldn't even be trying to hide how I feel about this, should I? Fine. It sucks. I hate it. I hate that I can't be the person you need me to be."

"Why can't you?"

She looked trapped. Hardwick tried again.

"I know they're your family. But they're terrible people."

"Only most of them." She gave a bitter laugh. "Some of them are only awful. One or two are pretty nice."

"So, keep those ones around. You don't need to live under your grandparents' thumb just because you share a family name. You're not even—"

"Don't. Don't say it." Delphine stood up, wringing her hands. "I'll go for that walk and let you rest."

"I wasn't going to say—"

"You should rest. Without me here. Shouldn't you?" She squared off against him, arms crossed, eyes blazing. "Is that the truth?"

"...Yes." Hardwick growled in defeat. "It is. I should rest."

"Alone."

"*No.*"

Delphine turned away, all business and angles and unhappiness as she gathered her jacket and outdoor gear. "Try to get some sleep. I'll call Jasper and see if he knows of any spare rentals around town. Or Jackson might be able to put you up. He and Olly are good people, I'm sure they'd be better at... all this... than any of my family."

"Delphine, wait. Please."

It was that last word that made her pause. She looked at him over her shoulder, her eyes shadowed with hope.

*You're not happy.* That's what he had been about to say. He'd thought that Delphine's desperate need to fit in with her family was because she had some sort of personal issue around not being a shifter, and she'd set her family up as some sort of flawless goal she wanted to be like, but that couldn't be true. She admitted her family was a pack of assholes. And she was miserable. All those lies she told, the whole fake life—and it left her miserable.

But he was in no position to ask questions. His head was spinning too badly for him to string more than a few words together. Even longer thoughts unraveled in his mind before he got to the end of them, torn away by the crashes of pain in his skull.

"Stay," he asked. "Please. Even if it hurts."

# 23

## DELPHINE

She stayed. How could she not?

*More like how* could *you,* she accused herself. *You should leave him. He'll be better off without you.*

His face was a rictus of pain. It wasn't fair, Delphine thought. It wasn't fair that someone could be that pale and close to passing out, and still hurting that much. Wasn't fainting meant to be a relief? But Hardwick seemed trapped, his body twisted from his so-called 'gift' and not even giving him the escape of unconsciousness.

"Tell me what you need," she begged. She bent over him, as though the pain he was experiencing was something external that she could protect him from. "Please. There has to be something I can do." *What is the point of me being his mate if all I do is cause him pain?*

"The truth," he gritted out. "Tell me something that is true."

Something true?

"I want to protect you," she whispered. Hardwick shuddered, but it was a shudder of relief, not pain. She stroked his hair, rested her hand on the back of his neck where the muscles were hard as stone. "I don't want you to hurt like this anymore. Or at all. I—"

She braced herself. The instinct to shy away from the truth was so embedded in her she had to force herself to peel away the lies that wrapped around it before the thought was even fully formed.

"—I'm a bit freaked out, how quickly I've come to care about you. I know that's how mate bonds work, but I've never had any sort of magic before. It's so new to me that it's terrifying. I want to be with you, but there's part of me that might run away at any second, because how can even magic make this work?"

*And you wanted me to run,* she added silently. *You wanted me to leave without saying anything. Without knowing the truth.*

Her words were easing something within Hardwick. His breathing became slower. The knife-like edges of his shoulder blades pressing through his shirt relaxed.

"Thank you," he whispered, his voice the last ragged edge of something almost worn through.

She stayed there, whispering nonsense until he was asleep—no, she reminded herself, not nonsense. True things. How she was worried he was overextending himself. How he should have told her that he was so much worse here than when they were alone. How she would have done something—she didn't know what, but *something*. Anything to keep him away from her family and the pain they caused.

It wasn't until she was certain he was asleep that she let the words that had been prickling in her throat out.

"I don't see how this is going to work," she whispered. His eyelids didn't even flicker. "You and me. Fate must have gotten it wrong. I don't even know who I am without the story I've told my family. How could I be good enough for you?"

When his breathing eased and she could move without risking waking him up, Delphine crept away and tried to call the people she knew who lived locally. No luck. Jasper wasn't picking up his phone, and neither was Jackson. Delphine left them both messages, outlining the situation in terms even more delicate than she would have used to extricate Mr. Petrakis from a disaster of his own making, and did not return to the hotel until much later that night. Until Hardwick had the rest he needed.

If he was asleep. God, she hoped he was. Not just because he needed it—though a better, less corrupted mate probably would have *only* wanted it for that reason. She wanted him to be asleep when she returned because she didn't want to return to the conversation that had hurt so much earlier.

She knew what he'd been about to say. And she didn't want to hear it.

That she wasn't a real Belgrave.

That everything she'd ever feared was true, and she was the weak link that would tear her family apart.

By the time she crept back into her room, Hardwick was dead to the world. She hoped he hadn't even noticed she was gone. And she waited by the doorway, watching him like a hawk, until she could convince herself that her presence wasn't hurting him even in his sleep.

She closed the door softly and tried not to feel as though she was breaking into her own room. She hadn't even been this self-conscious when she *actually* broke into Hardwick's life.

But she hadn't known what she did to him, then.

So she held her breath, and tip-toed, and brushed her teeth and changed into her pajamas, constantly on edge that she would make a noise, or bump into something, or that just the sheer power of her presence would be enough to drag Hardwick from his hard-won sleep.

Eventually, though, there was nothing else for it. She had to go to bed.

If only the hotel room had a sofa. Or even an armchair. The single desk chair crammed in one corner would be impossible to curl up in, but—maybe there was an extra blanket in the cupboard. She could camp out on the floor, or...

While she was dithering, she'd walked—*crept*—closer to the bed.

Hardwick was lying on his back. He had one arm thrown up over the pillow, and his face was the most peaceful she'd ever seen it.

Guilt twisted in her stomach. Of course she'd never seen him look peaceful. Because she'd always been *there*. Hurting him with her very presence.

And he hadn't said anything. Not until she'd forced it out of him.

*She* should have said more, today. She should have found some way to save him from having to meet her family. From having to see *her* around her family.

Without lying to them about *why* they needed to stay away.

That would be the trick. And that was another problem. If it *was* a trick, would it work, or would it only make Hardwick's condition worse?

If lying to help still hurt him, what was left?

She knew what he would say. *Tell the truth.*

Could she?

She looked down at him. The deep lines that etched his face had softened in sleep; he looked younger. Relaxed. She suddenly realized how constantly on edge he must be around other people. Whoever he was with, whatever they were talking about, he was just waiting for someone to stick a knife into his head and twist it.

He'd come all the way out here to recover after a year of using his abilities to help people, and she'd burst into his life like a custom-designed weapon.

She stepped closer. He didn't stir.

Maybe she could do better.

There had been a moment, hadn't there, when he'd looked at her without flinching? Not counting that incredible, exhilarating evening they'd spent making love. That couldn't count, she decided; it felt too unreal. Too raw and perfect. But after that, when they each knew the other's secret and before he'd started asking and asking her about her family, there had been... comfort.

She closed her eyes and focused on the light inside her. The mate bond—lodged in her heart, with the delicate strand of gold connecting her to Hardwick. Every time they'd touched, kissed, understood each other, it felt stronger.

But it was still so delicate.

She reached out to touch Hardwick's face and he rolled towards her, his hand coming up to hold hers.

He was still asleep. Still looking relaxed, and calm, and like it wasn't her at all that he was touching. Her heart filled her throat.

Not wanting to wake him up, she gently slid into the bed beside him. She tucked herself against his side, the same way she had earlier in the evening, before she figured out that what he really needed was for her to leave. But it was different now, wasn't it? He wasn't hurting.

Even if she had to leave before he woke up, she could stay now. Just for a while.

'Now' turned into all night, and in the morning, there was no time to escape.

"Delphine?"

Hardwick ran his hand down her back, softly, almost tentatively, as though he was trying to convince himself that she was really there. Delphine had been dreaming—she couldn't remember of what, just that it was soft, and easy, and the world felt right.

She opened her eyes and for a moment, her dream was real.

Hardwick was gazing at her with sleepy eyes. He looked as relaxed as he had done when he was asleep.

"You stayed," he murmured.

"I couldn't leave you here alone," she said at once. *On Christmas morning.* And just like that, the spell was broken. "I—I mean—maybe I should have—or I should have left before you woke up, that's what I meant to do—"

"Stop." His sleepiness was all gone now; he looked alarmed. She was getting this all wrong. Even when she tried to tell the truth, she got it wrong. "I'm glad you're here."

"Really?"

"Really." He pressed his forehead against hers and the shining mate bond in her heart glowed. "No lies, remember?"

And then he kissed her. His hands slid under her pajama shirt, caressing her waist and the tense line of her back.

She should have kept saying nothing. That seemed like the intelligent thing to do. Instead, when he finally pulled away, she asked:

"Do you feel better? Yesterday, you were—" *I was scared*, she wanted to say. But this wasn't about her.

He brushed a strand of hair off her face. "I won't tell you I'm feeling one hundred per cent, but I'm... improved." He snorted. "I could probably make it to breakfast without collapsing."

Breakfast. With her family. Her thoughts must have shown on her face because Hardwick rested a gentle hand on her cheek.

"Or not," he said. "Seeing as the thought of it makes you miserable."

"It's not only that. It's the thought of them hurting you, and…" And something so much more selfish she almost stopped herself from saying it. "And hurting me, too. After spending time with you and being able to tell you the truth about what I am, being around my family… It's so much work. And it feels as though I'm not me when I'm around them. I keep thinking, *None of you know me at all.* Maybe that's a good thing!" Even as she said it, it felt less like a joke and more like another horrible truth she had been keeping from herself. "When the truth does eventually come out, at least they won't all hate *me*. They'll hate the fake version of me I've been feeding them all these years."

"And who is the real version?"

"I—I don't know. I'm worried she doesn't exist, under all the lies." A hard bubble of laughter forced its way out of her throat. "That's the trick! I don't know what I'm worried about. How can I really be hurt by my family if I don't even really exist?"

"Delphine, you exist." Hardwick's caress was soft, but firm. "Of course there's a real you. I *know* you. You just need time to figure yourself out."

She shivered and pulled closer to him. "Not now."

"If you hate every minute of being with your family anyway, why not tell them? And you have me in your corner, now. You won't have to face them alone. Why not tell them today?"

"And ruin Christmas?"

"And finally have a Christmas you can enjoy on your own terms."

For a moment, the idea tempted her. A moment that made her light-headed with adrenaline. "No," she said quickly. "It's not only my secret to keep. And I'm not the only one who'll be hurt when it comes out. Not even the one who'll be the most hurt."

"I don't see how that's possible." Hardwick's voice was a possessive growl. "But it's your decision to make. In which case…" He rolled over, pulling her with him. "We don't need to see them at all. We stay here. Just us."

"I—" Delphine bit her lip. "I'm confused."

Stay here, instead of facing her family? Stay here, with the man who made her heart ache with joy and sorrow at the same time, instead of with the people who filled her with dread?

What was the catch?

Hardwick searched her face. Whatever he found there made his own eyes darken.

"I thought you wouldn't be here when I woke up," he admitted. "I thought you would think you had to leave for my own good. You would have reason to. I know that. I thought it myself, when I first met you, but I don't anymore."

"I wouldn't leave you to face my family alone." She traced the outline of his stubble.

"I would have escaped. Back into the mountains. Tried to fix the roof."

Delphine giggled. "You—you're not kidding. You don't lie. You really would have?"

"I'm hardy."

"It's still *freezing.*"

"Lions live in mountains like these, don't they?"

"Mountain lions."

"What about eagles?"

Delphine resettled herself on top of him. He was warm, and solid, and smiling at her as though she was the most wonderful person in the world, and she didn't want this perfect moment to end. This silly, pointless conversation that was somehow exactly what her heart had been crying out for.

"What if part of your griffin is happy in the cold and part isn't? What would you do then?"

"Some of the roof was still up when we left. I could put whatever bit of me didn't like the cold inside, and the rest could enjoy the view."

Laughter bubbled out of her. Hardwick smiled, and again, it transformed his face. She was happy. *He* was happy. This was how things were meant to be, wasn't it?

"I refuse to believe that you'd really do that."

"But you know it's the truth." He leaned up to kiss her. "And you know I can be hard-headed about things. Once I get an idea in my head, it's hard to get it to leave. I would have gone up there and tried to make it work. It would have been terrible." His smile broadened, and Delphine laughed again, and he kissed her again. He murmured against her lips: "Wouldn't have stopped me, though. I would have stuck it out. Until someone turned up to show me there was a better way."

"A better way?" she whispered back, her voice humming against his skin.

"With four walls and a roof. And someone who makes me complete."

She hesitated. Yes, a soulmate was meant to make someone complete. But—her? She hurt him. Everything she was, hurt him. Unless—

She could be someone else. Someone he needed. Someone who could help him, not hurt him.

She could be that person. She *would* be that person.

"Let's leave," she said suddenly, sitting up and straddling his waist. "Now. Before anyone else wakes up. Before—"

Something crashed into the window. Delphine yelped. Hardwick leapt up, getting between her and the window just as someone shouted outside.

Delphine pushed past Hardwick. "Is that—you have got to be kidding me. Anders?"

She strode across to the window. Her younger brother was dangling from the windowsill.

"Hey, sis," Anders said as she heaved the sash window open. "Happy Christmas?"

"What the hell, Anders? And where's Vance?" She leaned out the window, expecting to see the other twin hanging from another third-floor window.

"Up here!"

Vance was on the roof. Delphine's heart jumped. "What are you *doing*?"

"Having a better plan than Anders."

"A better plan for *what*?"

"Catching Santa."

"...*What*?"

Hardwick leaned out the window next to her, stared down at Anders and up at Vance, and raised one eyebrow. "Your brothers do this sort of thing a lot?"

"Unfortunately."

His eyelid flickered and she winced. It was a joke, not a lie, but she knew he was extra sensitive at the moment.

"Sorry."

"Don't be. It means you do like them, after all. Teenage dumbassery and all."

"Lucky them."

His eyes sparkled. "They are."

"Hey, you two wanna not take up the whole window? My fingers are gonna freeze off."

Hardwick's eyebrows pinched together as he stepped back. Delphine stuck to his side, slipping her hand into his. "So much for *just us*."

Anders vaulted up onto the windowsill using only his fingertips. He grinned at Delphine and Hardwick and dropped inside.

Delphine made an annoyed-older-sister noise. "You're not even wearing *shoes?*"

"Better toe-grip," Anders explained. There was a buzz at the back of her mind, and he rolled her eyes. "Trust Vance to take the lazy route. First, he doesn't even climb down the building, now he's still not climbing the building and he's just gonna walk down the stairs to get to your room?"

"Excuse me? How come my room is suddenly the place to hang out?"

"Oh, we, uh..." Anders trailed off.

Delphine crossed her arms and waited.

"Uhh..."

"Well?"

"Uhh..."

Someone knocked on the door.

"No guesses who that is." Hardwick strode over and unlocked the door. "Vance, right?"

"Future brother-in-law, right?" Vance nodded at Delphine as he sauntered in. "Hey, sis."

"Are either of you going to explain any of what you're doing?" Delphine demanded, exasperated. "*Santa?* You two do remember you're almost eighteen now, right?"

"You remember last year, right? The mystery of the Christmas cards?"

"It wasn't a *mystery*—"

"We left Christmas cards in a box in the woods, and on Christmas morning, someone had slipped them under the window! Ooh, mystery!"

"Hardly." Delphine explained to Hardwick: "One of the tourist businesses around here runs Christmas-themed sled dog trails where you can ride out to post a Christmas card in the woods. On Christmas Eve, the employees deliver the local cards around town. And the employees include an owl shifter and a *pegasus,* so I don't think you two need to literally stake out the hotel windows to figure out how they manage that without leaving tire tracks."

"Or it could be one of the dragons. Or the hellhounds! They work there too, don't they? Anyway, uh, that's not all we were doing." Anders nudged Vance. She saw a hint of sparkly cardboard hidden in his hand.

"You're stealing other people's Christmas post?" she gasped.

"No! Only ours! Uh, yours."

"Someone sent me a Christmas card?" She remembered doing this with the twins and her Mum the Christmas before. It had been a cute day out, with the twins pretending that racing dogsleds wasn't anywhere near as fun as flying. Who would have sent her a card this year? She couldn't imagine the twins going back—even if they had enjoyed themselves, it was more a thing for kids than for teenaged boys.

"Yeah, *we* sent it, sis."

Delphine shook her head slowly. "And now you're... stealing it back?"

Vance and Anders exchanged a nervous look. Anders pulled the card out of his sleeve where he'd hidden it. A cloud of glitter followed it. "We were going to leave it for you to read by yourself," he said, "Or, uh, not by yourself, I guess, but..."

Vance took up his trailing sentence. "We had second thoughts about how you would take it and thought it might, you know, help, if we were both here to explain."

Delphine's head buzzed, and she could only imagine the furious telepathic discussion her brothers were having. She crossed, thought again, and held out one hand.

"Go on, then. I have to read it before you can explain it, don't I?"

Reluctantly, Anders gave her the card.

More glitter fell off it as Delphine turned it over in her hands. It was exactly the sort of thing she remembered from last Christmas: a picture of Pine Valley, with a flying dogsled team howling 'Merry Christmas!' in glitter. She half-expected a tinny recording to start playing when she opened it.

Instead, her heart almost stopped.

It was Anders' handwriting. He'd written 'Happy Christmas sis!' at the top and something else smaller down the bottom, but it was the text in all-caps in the middle that made the blood turn to ice in her veins.

*Happy Christmas sis!* the card read, and then: *WE KNOW YOUR SECRET!*

# 24

# HARDWICK

Delphine went white. She sat down with a thump on the bed and Hardwick was standing between her and her brothers before he knew he'd started moving.

He shot the boys a warning look and knelt in front of her. Her knuckles were bone-white, clutched around the Christmas card so hard she was bending it out of shape.

"No," she whispered, her gaze so distant he knew she wasn't talking to him. "No, this can't be—"

Before Hardwick could say anything, the twins started talking over one another.

"I knew this was a bad idea!"

"You're the one who wrote it so it sounds more like a blackmail note than a Christmas card!"

"I thought it would be funny!"

Delphine dropped the card, her fingers suddenly unclenching like a piece of machinery. Hardwick picked it up. His face went stormy as he read it.

"This is meant to *not* be a blackmail note?" He doesn't bother to keep the growl from his voice.

"It says 'love from' us at the bottom!" Anders said plaintively. "And there's a winky face!"

"We should have *started* with that!" Vance hissed. "Dear sis, we love you, happy Christmas, we know your secret and we still love you—"

"That sounds even worse! It sounds like we *shouldn't* love her!"

"That's what you said the other day! And we ended up writing *that*!"

This could go on for hours, Hardwick thought. And someone would hear the shouting.

He interrupted them. "How about one of you tells us exactly what this message is meant to say, then." His griffin was angrier than he'd ever known it to be, and his voice had a sharp edge that was all claws.

Blessed Belgraves or not, the teenaged boys looked suitably awed. They exchanged another nervous look.

"You." Hardwick pointed at Vance. "The one who wasn't hanging off our windowsill. Talk."

He sat down next to Delphine. His griffin ached to transform and shelter her under its wing, but he made do with wrapping an arm around her. She leaned into his embrace, her spine stiff.

Hardwick watched Vance scramble for words. The young man stared at his sister, regret all over his face as he took in her frozen expression and twisted-together fingers.

"We're not stupid, you know," he blurted out.

Next to him, his brother groaned and bit down on his own hand. "Seriously?"

"Shit! That's not what I—I mean—after last year, when we surprised you here for Christmas and you didn't even want to talk to us—"

"That's not true!" Delphine's head jerked back. She glanced at Hardwick and, when he didn't react with pain, let her shoulders sag. Hardwick tightened his arm around her. Damn this family. They had her so messed up she couldn't even trust herself to say that she wanted to spend time with her own brothers without worrying that was a lie?

Delphine swallowed. "Of course I wanted to talk to you." About so many things, Hardwick guessed, even if she hadn't let herself acknowledge it. "You're my family. I—I thought I'd be spending Christmas with my boss, alone, and then you turned up, and I was so..."

She stopped.

Hardwick knew what she was going to say. It was obvious in the way her eyes had brightened as she got closer to the word, and how they'd shuttered over when she made herself hold her tongue.

Happy, he said to her silently. He didn't send the word telepathically; he held it close to his heart, pressed it into the golden light that joined his soul to hers. You were so happy.

"You were so *worried*." Vance sat down on the hotel room's squishy armchair by the window, suddenly looking a lot younger. "We thought you'd be happy, but the whole time we were here it was like you were tiptoeing around us. Like Mum does when we're at Grandma and Grandpa's. And—and we thought about how we hardly see you anymore. It's like you try to avoid hanging out whenever we're all together. Not just the big family parties, but even if it's just us."

"It's not like that." Delphine's face was tight with misery. "I love you guys. I really do. And Mum."

"And we love you too! That's why you should have told us you're not a shifter!"

There must have been some color left in Delphine's face after all because she went even paler. "I don't—what are you—"

"We figured it out, okay?" Anders' expression was sullen. Hardwick had enough experience with teens to know that it was because the kid was unhappy. "We should have figured it out earlier, but we didn't. Neither of us has ever seen you shift. You're way different when we talk over chat or video to when we talk in person. You're all interested in what we're doing, and stuff."

"Oh…" Delphine looked as though her heart was breaking.

"So, that's what the card's about." Anders was glaring at the carpet now. "We know you're not a shifter, but that's okay. Loads of people aren't shifters. And we still love you, or whatever."

Delphine's breathing had gone very quiet. "Does Mum know?"

"We haven't talked to her about it yet—"

"You can't tell her. You can't tell anyone." Any hint of softness in Delphine's body vanished. She was rigid as one of the frozen trees outside, all its sap turned to ice. "Promise me."

"But—"

"Promise!"

It was as close to a growl as he had ever heard from her. He wondered if the boys heard the desperation in it—or only the anger.

# 25

# DELPHINE

They promised not to tell. They didn't look happy about it, and Delphine knew she was being unreasonable, but fear tore at her under her skin until she'd browbeaten both of them into not saying anything.

"I can't go down to breakfast after that," she admitted to Hardwick after the twins had left, both of them sending her sullen, unhappy looks over their shoulders.

"If you don't want to go down, we're not going down." The protective growl in his voice made her heart quicken. "I'll reach out to the twins, tell them to say sorry, we can't make it. No one will think any less of you."

"On Christmas?"

"Your family seems… traditional. Can't see them complaining about your spending time with your new-found mate on Christmas morning."

Heat rushed through her at the claim in his words. *Your new-found mate.* That was what this should be like. Simple and perfect. But—

"You *cannot* say that to my brothers," she warned him. "I'll never hear the end of it."

She hesitated. There was a look on Hardwick's face like he wasn't saying something.

Her shoulders slumped. "Which would make a nice change from my relationship with them so far, which has been me not hearing… anything. I can't believe they figured me out."

"You okay?"

She shook her head slowly. "Yes? I am. I think. I feel awful that they thought I didn't care about them. But them knowing? If only I wasn't worried about them telling anyone, I would be… fine." Her lips twitched. "Maybe even better than fine. Maybe even good. Though that might be going too far."

Hardwick swept her hair behind one ear. "I don't think it would be going too far," he said gently. He pulled her into his arms, and his strength and careful, loving kisses did a better job of convincing her she might just be okay than her own heart did.

"Tell them," she decided at last. "We'll stay up here and get room service."

Someone knocked on the door. The back of Delphine's mind itched. She touched her head, frowning. "Do you hear that? Someone speaking telepathically?"

Hardwick shook his head and she sighed. That meant someone was speaking to her privately. But she couldn't know who without looking on the other side of the door, and without knowing who it was, she didn't know how to present herself when she opened the door...

The itch started up again. She motioned for Hardwick to stay where he was and cracked the door open, just a few inches. Enough so that she could glimpse who was behind it and arrange her face to be angry or bored or sleepily surprised, or—

"Mum?"

"Happy Christmas, sweetheart," Sara Belgrave said. "I didn't mean to interrupt. Are you almost ready to go down?"

Delphine wiped any trace of annoyance off her face and opened the door further. Her mother looked tired. She always looked tired when they were around the rest of the family—and she'd just had several days straight of them, in a town which the year before had been a relaxing sanctuary away.

"Ready? Hardly. We've just had the twins in here."

Her mother winced. "Oh dear. I'm sorry about that."

"They're too old and ugly now for you to take responsibility for everything they do, Mum."

"Good morning, Mrs. Belgrave." Hardwick came over to shake her hand, but Delphine's mother pulled him into a hug.

"Just 'Sara,' please."

"About breakfast—"

In the time it took Hardwick to work his way up to find a way to explain their plans to her mother that didn't suggest too strongly that they were going to stay in their room and bang, Delphine made a decision.

"We'll be right down," she said. "We just need to scrub up a bit first."

Was it her imagination, or did her mother look relieved? "I'll see you down there," she said. "I look forward to getting to know you better now that you're not under the weather, Hardwick."

"Likewise," Hardwick told her.

When her mother closed the door after herself, he turned to Delphine. "You changed your mind?"

"And I'm already wondering if it was the wrong decision." She shook her arms out, trying to relieve some of the nervous tension in her shoulders. And her neck. And her spine. And—

Hardwick's fingers pressed into her shoulders. He worked out the knots, his touch sure.

"I'm supposed to do this for you," she complained half-heartedly. "For your head."

"So, I don't just get treated that way when you're trying to find out my secrets?"

"Not only." Which she still felt bad about, but his voice was a warm purr, so she added: "I'd say it worked quite well, didn't it?"

He laughed into her hair. "Time for me to find out more of your secrets, then."

From the way his fingers trailed down her back—just firm enough to keep up the idea that this was a massage, just soft enough to hint at something else—the *secrets* he was referring to were not of the deep, psychological kind. She took a step backwards. He followed, his thumbs slipping down to rub teasing circles around her tailbone; she stepped again, he followed again, until they were in the bathroom.

And then it all went wrong. Hardwick was as enticing as he had been before, his dark eyes sensuous, his hands wickedly teasing—but Delphine was too distracted to let herself be distracted. She couldn't drag her mind away from the breakfast table downstairs, the idea of her relatives all gathering together, what possible plan of attack she could formulate to keep them from hurting Hardwick with their thoughtless lies—and her brothers. She might not have spent as much time with them as she should have, or wanted to, but she knew them.

She knew that if she wasn't there to steer the conversation and deal out a few well-timed kicks, she couldn't trust them to keep their mouths shut. Not if they thought they were helping her. God, if they did that—

Clean, dampish, and thoroughly dissatisfied, she and Hardwick made their way downstairs at the same time as her cousins Brutus and Livia. Livia was complaining about having to wait until after breakfast to open presents. They both gave Hardwick a piercing look and asked him if he was feeling better. He was polite enough, but for the first time, Delphine wanted to put her hands in the center of Brutus's stupid chest and shove him away.

"Merry Christmas to you, too," he murmured as they hurried off.

"I'm sorry," she said, her voice as low as his.

"Looks like it's hunting season for poor, weak, headache-suffering griffins." He kissed her. "I'm happy to take the heat if it means keeping it away from you."

Christmas breakfast. In movies and books, it was the first moments of magic—families slowly waking up, kids squealing over stockings, early risers shaking and tapping wrapped gifts trying to figure out what was inside. Sometimes it was skipped over altogether in a festive whirl of fun and happiness.

Christmas breakfast in the heart of the Belgrave clan...

Delphine's heart broke a little more as she realized how she had wasted her previous Christmas with her family. Last year, they'd had a quiet, relaxing breakfast, just the four of them. Anders had tried to make pancakes, and Vance had snuck out while the smoke alarm was blaring to buy pastries from a bakery that was open early morning for exactly that sort of Christmas emergency.

And all the time she'd been hiding herself. Being Delphine-the-terrible-sister rather than Delphine-the... whatever she really was.

The dining room was set up the same way it had been the evening before, with all the tables that would normally be arranged separately for different groups to eat alone pushed together into one long table. There was a red table runner running the length of the mega-tablecloth, decorated with wreaths of pine and holly and dotted with tealight candles in cute holders. The candlelight glinted on champagne glasses and water carafes and the round belly of the bottle of port Delphine had bought for her grandfather, which was sitting in pride of place in front of her grandparents.

The seating arrangement was so familiar it might have been a snapshot from any Christmas of her childhood. Her grandmother and grandfather were seated at the head of the table, with her other relatives arrayed down either side according to how much her grandparents wanted to lecture them, peer at them, or test their knowledge of Belgrave family history. Once upon a time, Delphine had thought that her grandparents ordered the family meals based purely on most to least liked, top to bottom of the table. Favored aunts and uncles at the top, sneered-upon relations at the bottom. But it wasn't that simple. The bottom of the table was as coveted as the top of the table. It was the middle that was the dead zone. Hemmed in on either side by loud conversation, unable to focus on anything without someone passing a dish over your plate or spilling gravy in your drink—*that* was where the least favored Belgraves were banished to. Including Delphine's family.

She'd always had mixed feelings about that. On the one hand, it was horrible. She hated that ever since Delphine's father had died, her mother had been so obviously excluded. On the other, it meant they paid less attention to her little corner of the family as a whole. And she was despicably grateful for that.

Delphine took a deep breath and wrapped her arm through Hardwick's. "Let's sit with my folks," she said. "It shouldn't be as bad as last night."

She checked his face warily. Did wishful thinking count as a lie?

"And we can keep an eye on your brothers," he murmured back, closing his hand over hers reassuringly.

His comfort gave her the strength to stride into the room and greet the people she walked past. To her relief, the seats closest to the head of the table were already filled. She nodded to a couple of spare seats further down, sitting opposite her brothers. Far enough from the head of the table that they wouldn't have to be part of any conversations up there, but not so far that her grandmother would peer down and demand to know what they were doing so far away. Her brothers waved her over.

Before they could sit down, however, her grandfather's voice cut through the hum of conversation.

"Is that Delphine? Come down here and tell me what you've been doing with yourself, girl."

# 26

# HARDWICK

Hardwick sensed rather than saw Delphine's shoulders go up. Because they didn't move. Because she'd been dealing with these people all her life, and must have learned long ago not to let her true feeling show.

He had braced himself as they entered the breakfast room, but there was no need. He felt stronger than he had the night before. Stronger than he had in months. Something Delphine had said—

Her words came back to him, wrapping around him like her embrace.

*I want to protect you.*

Nobody had ever wanted to protect him. Not since his parents passed. His gift, and the pain it brought with it, had been his alone to bear. He had thought that if he ever found his mate, it would be his job to be the sole provider, the protector, the one who defended her against every danger the world had to offer. The thought that she would want to protect him, too, had never occurred to him. And now the knowledge that Delphine wanted to look after him, to *care* for him, formed a shield around his heart. His griffin was content, despite the conversation around them.

Because the Belgraves were sure as hell playing the same social bullshit games they'd been on the night before.

Everyone had slept terribly or had some complaint or other about the hotel's heating, cooling, the service of their staff, the noise from the street outside. It was all lies, and it all washed off his shield like water off a duck's back. His griffin pecked half-heartedly at a few of them, and there was a dull ache in his head like something was getting through, but it was nowhere near the agony that had spiked through his skull the previous evening.

He remembered their conversation about his griffin's sign language. She'd said it must make it harder to lie, but wasn't that what she was doing right now? It didn't make his head hurt, but it—

His griffin narrowed its eyes at him.

Of course. This wasn't lying. It was self-defense.

Delphine gave him the strength to be here. In return, he would do whatever he could to get them through this day without her being hurt.

By anyone. Including her brothers.

Hardwick eyed each of Delphine's relatives as they made their way to the head of the table. He nodded, and smiled, and muttered 'Good morning' and 'Merry Christmas' whenever anyone met his deceptively mild gaze.

Her aunts and uncles wouldn't be out of place at a country club, he thought. At least not the sort he'd encountered while he was on the job. Wealthy, well-groomed, and completely assured of their own importance. *Did they have country clubs in England?* he wondered.

The younger generation looked to be going the same way. All polished, military-grade self-esteem. But...

His gaze lingered on one of Delphine's cousins and her mate. Pebbles, he wanted to say her name was, though what the hell sort of Flintstones name was that? And her mate—something else beginning with P. The bird of paradise shifter.

Something niggled at the back of his mind. If he'd been at work, he would have followed it to its source, figured out what connection his subconscious was trying to make while his conscious mind was dreaming of painkillers and icepacks.

But he wasn't at work. It was Christmas morning, he was on holiday, and right now his top priority was looking after his mate.

He stuck close to Delphine as she made her way to the head of the table. Anders and Vance tried to tag along behind them, but their grandmother waved the two of them away with an "I've seen enough of *you* two already. Go sit with your cousins."

She waved Grizelda and Michael away, too and ushered Delphine and Hardwick grandly into their abandoned seats. Hardwick held Delphine's chair for her and got a grandmotherly smirk for his troubles.

"Good morning, Grandmother, Grandfather," Delphine said. "Did you sleep well?"

Alastair sniffed. "Hrm! You'd think this place has rats in the walls, the amount of noise there was this morning."

"I'm sure they do their best," Angela said. To the untrained ear, it probably sounded like she was trying to smooth over troubled waters, not insult their hosts. The lie skated across the backs of Hardwick's eyeballs. "And I do hope you're feeling better today, Mr..."

"Jameson. Hardwick Jameson."

"Of course." Her grandmother's eyes went distant, and given what Delphine had told him, he guessed she was sifting through her memories for any noteworthy Jamesons. Noteworthy, in Angela Belgrave's book, meaning with a pedigree going back at least five hundred years and ideally an ancestor who had been immortalized in local folklore somewhere across the globe.

*Good luck to her*, Hardwick thought. If the Jamesons made a name for themselves doing anything, it would be keeping to themselves—and that was the sort of thing where if you became known for it, you weren't very good at it.

"I was terribly sorry to hear you were ill. I had hoped we could have proper introductions last night."

"Well, no time like the present." He slid into the chair next to Delphine and took her hand under the table. Her fingers were stiff.

"Indeed." Angela took a delicate sip of iced water and fell silent as one of the hotel staff came around and took their breakfast orders. Hardwick was impressed. She didn't even speak telepathically, that was how determined she was not to talk in front of the 'help.'

Delphine's grandfather took up the conversation once the waitstaff had moved away.

"Now, what it is you do, Hardwick?"

Hardwick started to explain his job and where he worked, but the old man talked over him.

"No, no, not your employment. My God!" He leaned forwards. "I'm not interested in your job. What do you *do*? We Belgraves, we winged lion shifters, we're all about family. If I look into your soul, Hardwick—and you don't mind if I do?"

Hardwick shrugged and held Mr. Belgrave's eye. He got a glimpse of the other man's lion—stern, stubborn, and boastfully proud—and his own griffin peered out through his eyes, allowing itself to be seen.

Alastair leaned back and slapped the table, a satisfied smirk on his lips.

"Well, that tells me *what* you are. But being one of the gifted ones doesn't set you apart from the crowd these days. It's what you *do* with it that counts. Take our family, for example. Winged lion shifters. What does that tell you?"

"Just what it says on the tin, sir."

Mr. Belgrave slapped the table again. "Did you hear that, Angela? Just what it says on the tin! That is exactly what I'm talking about, m'boy. Modern shifters don't pay enough attention to the important things. Nothing about intention. Nothing about *why* we are the way we are."

*Save me*, Hardwick thought, fixing a noncommittal, neutral look on his face. He'd encountered shifters like this before. Mostly when they were trying to explain that they'd robbed someone, or smashed something, or both, as a result of their unique shifter nature. They always seemed to think that because he was a shifter too, he'd let them off. As though animal instincts were something to proud of, let alone an excuse.

"That *why*," Mr. Belgrave went on, "is what separates shifters like us from the normal type."

Well, that was a new direction, at least. An exciting new distillation of a perspective he already disliked.

But this was Delphine's family, and he was there for her, not to let his own biases show.

He could put up with some shifter posturing, for her sake.

"So, what is your *why*, Mr. Belgrave?"

"Family. That's the *why* of the Belgraves. It's all about family. You were talking with my girl Grizelda last night, weren't you? She understands it. Our son Dominic did, too, before he passed."

Delphine stiffened. Hardwick touched the back of his hand to her arm. "My father," she explained quickly.

"Passed when the twins were babies and Delphine here was only a girl herself, poor thing," her grandmother added. "Such a shame that he didn't live long enough to see her greater form. That was just before your lioness emerged, wasn't it, dear?"

Delphine looked stricken. She very carefully did not look at Hardwick, though she squeezed his hand. "Just after," she said quietly.

It wouldn't have mattered if she'd whispered it. It hurt all the same. Worse than before, as though the few minutes they'd spent together when she wasn't lying about herself had weakened his defenses. Even the background conversation thudded more heavily against his mind.

"—of course, we're *so* excited—"

The same as the night before. *Worse* than the night before.

"—invited all the *best* shifter families to her First Flight, our darling Livia simply wouldn't have it any other way—"

"—really, it was a blessing in disguise. I'm afraid that the Eastern dragons simply aren't all they're cracked up to be—"

Lie upon lie. Shifters who claimed that family was the most important thing, then spent all the time they had together faking it. Most of them hated being here. The sheer volume of lies about how happy they were that the family was all together was proof of that. Cousin Livia wasn't interested in the 'best shifter families,' whoever *they* were. And Hardwick wouldn't have been surprised if the Eastern dragons had seen right through Grizelda Belgrave's bullshit and decided to have none of it.

These were the people Delphine was so desperate to keep on board?

He forced himself to focus on what she was saying, and not let himself be drawn into the lesser blows to the skull from the rest of the table.

"...So, he did know about my lioness," Delphine said, glancing at Hardwick with a barely-there

I'm-sorry look before smiling peacefully at her grandmother. "I was so happy to be able to tell him before he passed."

"We know." Mrs. Belgrave's smile out-beatified Delphine's like the sun outshines a lightning bug. "But it is good to hear you tell the story, dear. Goodness knows it's the one bright point in that whole sad affair."

"And the boys," her husband added. It sounded like an old bit of patter.

"And the boys, of course. Belgraves through and through."

Hardwick took that as his cue to check what the boys were up to. He'd hoped to find them deep in another trivial argument, like the day before, or—damn. His brain put two and two together. The night before, in the lead-up to his breakdown, the twins had been causing a ruckus. Hardwick had put it down to teenage dumbassery, but they'd only started throwing candles when the all-knowing Grizelda had started talking about...

Shit.

He glared at them both and sent them a silent warning. They glared back. Not a good sign, he thought, even as he begrudgingly respected them for daring it.

After all, though, who was he? Some interloper who barely knew the first thing about the Belgrave family history. Who, to their eyes, must be encouraging their sister to keep hiding behind her pretense at being something she wasn't. A pretense that clearly made her miserable. They had to have seen how unhappy she was, back in the hotel room.

Just like it was obvious to anyone with half a brain that she was tense now, too. And the twins, candle-tossing or not, had at least half a brain between them.

How long until their Belgrave family-above-all instincts won out and they tried to protect her from her grandparents' assumptions about who she was?

Hardwick's griffin clacked its beak nervously. He realized at the same moment that his head was aching less. He'd managed to tune out the rest of the table—as a result of his focus on Delphine?

But that wasn't why his griffin was nervous. Mr. and Mrs. Belgrave weren't lying. They really believed that Delphine's lioness emerging had helped her and the rest of the family deal with the pain of losing their son. That it balanced the scales, somehow.

Even more unsettled, his griffin wrapped itself around the bright glow of the mate bond, whipping its tail.

"So." Mr. Belgrave turned back to Hardwick. "Now that you understand what I'm asking, what do you say? What is a griffin's *why*?"

And Hardwick, bristling, went as much on the offense as he could manage without betraying his mate.

"Funny thing, you asking me about my *why*. I was going to say the concept had never occurred to me, but I realize it has. I've been living it for years without ever putting it into words." He thought about the last ten years: the decisions he'd made. The wins. All the work he'd achieved. "I'm all about helping people. My gift, as you put it, lets me do that. I use it to keep people safe."

"So that's what griffins are about, is it?"

"It's what this griffin is about."

Mrs. Belgrave gave a tinkling laugh.

The doors to the dining room opened, and several members of the hotel staff came in wheeling trolleys of food. Mrs. Belgrave pinched her lips in ostentatiously. *I was beginning to wonder where our breakfast was! Honestly, they call this service?*

Hardwick called it damn good service. They'd only made their orders a few minutes before, and the dishes looked freshly cooked, not like they'd been sitting under a warmer slowly drying out. His stomach rumbled as the server set a plate of crispy bacon and mounds of scrambled eggs in front of him. Even the greens on the side looked fresh. Nothing like the pre-cooked, re-heated rubbish he'd been planning to dine on the whole holiday.

"This looks better than those enchiladas," he said to Delphine.

"Significantly better. The coffee's nicer, too."

"You mean it's actually drinkable?"

She smiled, and just before she turned away to accept her own plate of food, her smile changed. It became a little less amused, and a little more honest. A pocket of realness between the two of them, amidst all her family's insincerity.

Then she replied to something her grandmother said, and it changed again, back into the pleasant, utterly insincere expression that she wore around all of her older relatives. Hardwick frowned.

"Keeping people safe. Well, I'm sure there are worse things to dedicate your soul to," Mr. Belgrave joked. He waved a fork at Hardwick. "Almost a shame you're paired with Delphine, though. Belgraves don't need saving as a rule."

A vision of Delphine out cold in the snow flashed into Hardwick's mind, and his griffin's crest rose angrily. "That so?"

At the other end of the table, a pocket of silence fell. If Hardwick hadn't been keeping an ear on the twins, he wouldn't have noticed it.

"We keep to tradition with many things, but the whole damsel in distress thing is so passé," Mrs. Belgrave said. "A true lioness would never let herself get into a situation where she was reliant on anyone else."

Her eyes flicked down the table. Hardwick didn't see who she was looking at, but Delphine went tense.

"No, we're all about the saving, aren't we, Grandmother? Oh," she added. "And the family, Grandfather. I can't forget that."

"I guess that makes saving family the ultimate twofer." Hardwick was struggling to keep his temper under control. They would have left her. They wouldn't have even bothered to look for her. She could have died out there, and her family would have been here, laughing and congratulating themselves on how powerful and family-oriented they were. "Seems like a hard bet if your family members never need to be saved."

"Hardwick—" Delphine hissed under her breath. Her hand found his and squeezed it tight. "Don't—"

"Not *exactly*, my dear," Mrs. Belgrave said, the words dropping from her mouth like poison. She looked down the table again and then shut her eyes, like a martyr praying for strength. "*True* Belgraves would never need to be saved, of course. I would be happy to count those who marry into the family in that, but I'm afraid that history—"

"Hey," Anders called out. "Are you talking about our dad?"

"Would anyone like some more coffee?" Delphine said desperately.

"—history is against us in that respect. And thus, sadly, Belgraves may indeed find ourselves called upon to save other Belgraves. Whatever the cost."

"And without weighing up whether the possible benefits are worth it."

Outrage roared against the inside of Hardwick's skull. It wasn't the pain of lies—it was a telepathic scream, as wordless and intense as dragonling Cole's had been when he was caught in the snow. Even Delphine winced and hissed in a breath.

Her eyes flew to his. "What was—oh, no."

Anders and Vance were both standing up, their faces stormy. "What do you mean, *possible benefits?*" Anders growled.

Opposite them, their mother tried fruitlessly to reach across the table and tug them back down into their seats. Hardwick couldn't hear her whispered pleas, but he got the gist.

The two elder Belgraves stared at the commotion with equally disdainful expressions. "I meant exactly what I said," Alastair sniffed.

"Yeah, which is? Come on. If you're going to say it, say it!"

"No..." Delphine whispered. Hardwick stood up and touched her shoulder.

"All right," he said out loud, pitching his voice to convey rationality and level-headedness, "let's hold off a minute and stay calm, not-"

"All I am saying is—don't look at me like that, Delphy, if she didn't want to hear it then she should have kept your brothers in line—is that if one *is* going to save someone, it's best to think of the overall benefit of that, versus the risk. Now, I'm not saying that Dominic wasn't—"

"FUCK YOU!"

Vance launched himself down the table. He flattened one of his cousins face-first into his breakfast, and sent glasses and water jugs flying.

"How dare you!" he yelled. "You've always treated our Mum like you were ashamed of her, and now you say Dad should have let her die? You talk so much shit about family and it's all lies!"

"You don't care about family at all!" Anders had grabbed Vance, but he seemed more interested in making sure he had his own say than stopping his twin from fighting his way down the table. The others on that side of the table were standing up, now, trying to hold the teenagers back. "Everyone hates you but they're too scared to say it! No wonder Delphy doesn't want to tell you she's not a shifter!"

Silence fell. Delphine staggered, as though the silence had hit her physically. Vance turned around and pulled Anders into a headlock with his arm over his mouth. Too late.

Then the whispers started.

"Pretend to be a shifter?"

"What's he saying?"

"But Delphy *is* a... isn't she?"

"She never had a First Flight."

"Her father had just died!"

Mr. Belgrave drew himself up. "Yes. Your father had just died, Delphine. Our only son. Perfect timing for you, was it? Giving up your First Flight, hiding yourself in your studies..."

"It wasn't like that!" Delphine protested. Which was the truth.

"You lied to us all." Her grandmother's voice quavered artistically. Hardwick got the feeling she wasn't surprised at all. There was something in her eyes that was more triumphant than shocked.

Delphine was shaking. Her eyes twitched from side to side, hunting for a way out. When she found it, she let out a ragged sob. "Fine. I lied." The words sounded like they were being torn out of her. "It's—it's exactly what Hardwick said. I lied because I knew you'd never accept me if I wasn't a shifter. I lied to—to protect myself."

*Lies.* Hardwick jerked. His griffin leaned forward, tearing at the sentences with its beak.

*I lied.*

True.

*I lied because I knew you'd never accept me if I wasn't a shifter.*

True.

*I lied to protect myself.*

Lie.

Hardwick felt as though a rug had been pulled from under him. All this time he'd assumed she was lying to secure her own place in the family. But if she wasn't lying to protect herself, who was she trying to protect?

His mind echoed with the pressure of a dozen frenzied psychic conversations going on at once. Even adults lost their fine control of telepathic speaking when they were upset. But two voices cut through the others, directly to Hardwick's mind.

*Tell her I'm sorry, I'm sorry I'm so sorry—*

*He didn't mean it, please tell her that, neither of us were going to say anything we promise—*

Delphine's brothers sounded close to tears. But he didn't have time for them. Delphine had staggered to her feet, her face bone-white.

"Let's just go," she muttered, her voice broken. She rubbed her hands through her hair, her fingers digging at her scalp. "Everyone's—I can't—please, I have to leave."

"Don't be so hasty, Delphine." Her grandmother's voice was sickly-sweet. "You were only a child."

"Oh, God." Delphine closed her eyes. She clenched her fists and turned slowly back to her grandparents. Hardwick watched her pull herself together vertebra by vertebra, gathering her fragmented dignity to herself. "I was old enough to know what I was doing, Grandmother. And it's not like I ever stopped. I lied! Blame me!"

"But isn't there someone else we *should* be blaming, Delphy?"

"No one," she gritted out.

"It's not your fault you're not a shifter, after all."

# 27

# DELPHINE

No. This couldn't be happening.

Delphine tried her best to erase the last thirty seconds from her memory. As though ignoring it would mean it hadn't happened. As though she could stop her skull from rattling as half her family tried to shout at her telepathically and wipe away the looks of horror and disgust on every face she turned to.

"How long have you known?" Her grandfather's voice cracked like a whip.

Delphine's throat worked. What was the best thing to do? Keeping the peace wouldn't work anymore. There was no peace to keep.

And she couldn't lie. She didn't let herself glance at Hardwick, but she felt his presence beside her and in her heart. The memory of his face going grey under the onslaught of Belgrave boasting was fresh in her mind.

No peace. No lying.

Just one chance, if she was lucky, to stop the real truth from escaping after all this time.

She stuck her chin out. *Be fierce. Be arrogant. Be a Belgrave, for the last time in your life.* "Trying to figure out how long I fooled you?"

"How long you've been lying to us!"

"What, your Belgrave family-ing didn't clue you in all this time?" She tossed her hair—actually tossed her hair, like the feisty governess in one of her grandmother's novels. "I'm surprised. There were a few years, before I left for uni, that I thought you'd figured it out and were keeping quiet to try and salvage the family honor, or something."

"How dare you!" her grandfather bellowed, which was wonderfully to plan even if it did make her want to run and hide, but her grandmother was worryingly clear-eyed.

"Alastair," she murmured, and her husband reined himself in. "You know, we really can't *blame* her. Even now, she's only trying her best to distract us from the real problem, the poor dear."

"You absolutely can blame me." Delphine spoke through gritted teeth.

One of the angry bees buzzing against her mind stopped. A second later, Anders shouted: "I'm sorry! I was just trying to protect—"

"Protecting your *family,* is it?" Her grandmother raised her eyebrows. "It appears that there is a bit of that going around. As though proper Belgraves ever needed to be *protected*. Of course, now it's all out in the open. We all know exactly how much of a Belgrave—"

"I'm not protecting anyone but myself!" Delphine snapped before she could get any further.

She was only thinking of one person, then, and of the raw, torn emptiness that had opened up inside her when her brother yelled out her secret.

Hardwick choked off a curse. His hand came down heavily on her arm, and the back of his own chair. She spun to support him, and by the time she turned back to glare at her grandparents and try to get the conversation back on track, it was too late.

Eyes were darting towards her mother. Grizelda. Martin. All the other relatives whose names and habits she'd painstakingly memorized over the years. Even the younger generation. Pebbles looked like she was going to be sick. She was gripping her mate's hand, white-knuckled.

Delphine's heart felt like Pebbles' hand. Straining and bloodless.

How had she ever thought she could bluff her way through this? She knew how her family worked. She knew what Belgraves *were*. There was nothing more important to them than family... and now they all knew the truth about her, they knew she didn't deserve to be called family.

She wasn't a winged lion.

She wasn't even a shifter.

How could she be a Belgrave?

"Mum—" Her voice was a creak. A wisp.

Her mother was standing silently further down the table. She was staring straight at Delphine. Staring at her in a way she hadn't since—since—

Since the day Delphine's father died.

Her grandmother sneered. "I always said that Dominic should have—"

"*Angela,*" her grandfather said, in a fond sort-of-telling-off way that Delphine knew was nothing of the sort. He wanted her to keep talking. He just wanted the appearance of not being one hundred percent ready to let his wife rip into their daughter-in-law.

Her grandmother turned her eyes back to her. "You poor, deceitful girl." Her gaze was sickly sweet and full of pity, and her lioness stared out, viciously triumphant. "You lied to us. All of us. After Dominic died, we took you in. Treated you like our own, like a real Belgrave, when all this time you were worse than a cuckoo in our nest! And *you!*"

She turned to Delphine's mother.

"Are you happy now? First you took our son away, and now you've destroyed the entire Belgrave bloodline! Centuries of history, gone!"

"She didn't know!" Delphine cried out.

Everyone turned to face her. Even Hardwick.

Delphine could have sobbed.

Of course her mother didn't know. How could she? Delphine had done all of this to protect her.

And now she would hate her for it.

Around the table, her relatives' faces were twisting with disgust. Uncle Martin and Aunt Grizelda edged away from her. The younger cousins, Livia and Brutus, looked almost as excited as Grandmother. Her brothers—she couldn't even look at them.

Her mind itched. Pebbles was staring at her like she'd broken her heart.

"This is Auntie Sara's fault," Pebbles announced, her voice shaking. She stuck her chin out and glared down the table at Delphine's mother, who still hadn't said anything. "You should have said something—if we'd *known*—"

Delphine's spine bristled. She could take them attacking her. But not her Mum.

"She didn't know anything about it!" Her fists clenched as she willed Pebbles to look at her. "And what would you have done differently, if you'd known I turned out not a shifter?"

Fury blazed from Pebbles' face. "I would have—I would have—"

"What? Not married Pascal?"

Pebbles reeled back. Beside her, Pascal's eyes flicked nervously from Belgrave to Belgrave. "I wouldn't have brought him back here at least!"

"*Penelope!*"

It had been so long since anyone used Pebbles' real name, even she took a moment to realize their grandmother was talking to her.

Angela was irate. "Dominic was bad enough, but he was always a dreamer. I thought you of all people would understand the importance of sacrificing for this family!"

"I'm sorry? Pascal is my *mate!*"

"Don't be so naïve, girl," Alastair rasped. "Do you think fate has blessed our family all these years because we let it control our lives?"

"But you always said fate was kind to us." Pebbles' eyes went wide.

Suspicion prickled on the back of Delphine's neck. Pebbles glanced at her and for a moment their eyes met. Her mind itched, and it didn't take years of practice to guess what Pebbles was trying to say to her, already forgetting that her non-shifter cousin couldn't hear her.

"What are you saying, Grandfather?" Delphine asked carefully.

"Fate is kind to us," Alastair announced pompously, "because we know when to follow it, and when to *ignore* it. Your grandmother and I aren't mates, but we—"

Chaos. That was the only word for it. Every Belgrave started shouting at once.

All except two.

"—we did what was *right* to preserve the Belgrave *line*!" Alastair roared.

Delphine hardly heard him.

The arguing voices turned into angry shouts. Delphine took an automatic step back and almost tripped over her chair. Hardwick steadied her and she leaned against him, the light in her chest flickering at the same pace as the thudding of her heart.

"I thought it would just be me," she whispered to him. "I didn't think it would destroy my whole family."

Her mother was still staring at Delphine.

And she looked terribly, terribly sad.

Delphine grabbed Hardwick's hand. He turned to her at once, his dark eyes searching hers.

"Hardwick—" she began.

His eyebrows drew together. "We're leaving?"

She nodded.

It wasn't running away, she told herself as she and Hardwick slipped out and the other Belgraves screamed at each other. She was just getting a head start on being thrown out of the family. The family she'd always told herself she was doing this for.

It was only as the cold Christmas air hit her face outside that she started to cry.

# 28

# HARDWICK

Hardwick followed Delphine out into the street. He wished he could say they were striding out together, but even with his arm around her shoulders, he could feel the distance between them. An icy shell forming around her, protecting her shattered heart.

He should be the one to protect her. But she had spent so long alone. She didn't know how to let him in. How to trust him to hold her heart and keep it safe while she was hurt.

Just like he hadn't known how to trust her, when they first met.

He wrapped one arm around Delphine's shoulders, searching his pockets for a clean handkerchief with the other. But no matter how closely he held her, he felt as though he was losing sight of her.

The plaza outside was merrily bedecked with Christmas decorations. The hotel was on Pine Valley's main square, the hub of all the Christmas bustle that had driven Hardwick away only a few days ago. Today, the place was almost completely deserted. A white-feathered bird settling its wings in a tree was the only sign of life.

Strings of light glimmered in shop windows, and sparkling tinsel was wrapped around every streetlamp and power line. A cluster of Christmas trees huddled in the middle of the square, surrounded by locked-up food carts and abandoned picnic tables decked out like Santa sleighs.

It was the ghost town Hardwick imagined when Jackson first told him about Pine Valley, and it was the most miserable thing he'd ever seen.

Delphine muttered something under her breath and ducked away from Hardwick's embrace. She walked away from him. His arm fell to his side, leaden.

She hadn't looked at him since they left the building. He couldn't get a read on her. She was too good at hiding the truth in her body language. In her winter jacket, with the furred hood hiding the tilt of her head and the quilted fabric obscuring the set of her shoulders and her spine, she was a blank slate.

Hardwick's griffin was desperate to connect with her. It hovered its wings around the glowing mate bond in Hardwick's chest, like someone trying to protect a candle flame from the wind. And it made sharp, pecking motions at Hardwick himself, urging him to go to her.

He was too scared to move.

When he thought of calling out to her, his throat went dry. Each breath he inhaled seemed to chill his whole body and the silence left after the shouting in the breakfast room echoed in his ears.

*Say something,* he told himself. *For God's sake, it's Christmas, and you just watched her family tear itself apart. Say something!*

"Delphine—"

"Were they lying?"

"What?"

Delphine's voice was slightly muffled. "In there. Everyone who was yelling. My grandparents, Pebbles… were they lying?"

"No." Hardwick's shoulders slumped.

Delphine gave a damp chuckle and wiped one hand across her face. She was still looking away, but Hardwick was putting two and two together now. Her carefully even breaths. The dampness in her voice.

"You're crying," he said, stupidly.

Delphine hiccupped. "I'm not—I am, but it's just—" She raised both hands to her face and let them fall with a gasp of frustration. "It's nothing I didn't expect."

The truth in those five words made Hardwick's teeth ache.

"I'm sorry," he said. "I should have protected you better. I meant what I said to your grandfather, about being the sort of person who helps people. I thought I was helping you by standing by your side, but I should have seen the risk. You told me you wanted—"

"—I wanted to stop feeling everyone's expectations on me. Shaping me. Making me into something I'm not. Or might not be." She wrapped her arms around herself, still staring out towards the Christmas trees. There was a long, icy silence. "I don't know if that is what I wanted, now."

"Delphine, I'm so sorry. I…"

"Stop." She turned around. Her eyes were red, and there were flecks of tears on her cheeks that she hadn't yet wiped away, but her expression was determined. "I'm not angry at you. I'm not—I don't even know if I'm angry at Vance and Anders. I'm… angry at myself."

"That's worse," he growled, and she snorted.

"I've been such an idiot. I thought I was doing this for my family. For—for the Belgrave family name, or something. That's what I told myself. For *years*! And now it's all out in the open, and that was all a lie. I let the twins walk right into my grandfather's trap. It's my fault. I was only trying to save myself the whole time, not even thinking about what they would go through. And I don't care what my grandmother or grandfather say at all, or my aunts and uncles, only—"

She stopped and her eyes filled with tears. He pulled her to him at once and she leaned into him, pressing all her weight against his as though she wanted his hug to swallow her whole.

"Mum looked at me like I'd broken her heart. She didn't even say anything. I know—I know I've been lying to them all this whole time. I *know* that. I just…"

She buried her face against his chest.

"I didn't expect it to hurt so little with the rest of them and so much with her," she said miserably. "I want—I've always wanted it not to be true, what I am, because it means that everything she and Dad were fighting for when they got together was wrong, after all. Them being together didn't magically turn out all right. Dad died, and I'm not even a real Belgrave. Even if the twins are, I'm… broken. And I wanted… I wanted…"

She clung to him, desperation in every word. And truth. Hardwick's heart ached for her. He'd wanted to save her—but how could he save her from this?

His griffin strained to find a hint of untruth in what she was saying. Nothing. Delphine was telling the truth, just as he'd wanted, and it was breaking his heart.

All her lies had been to protect herself, after all. And she hadn't even realized it.

"I wanted my mother to still love me, even if nobody else did. How can she? The way she was looking at me. She's ashamed of me. *I'm* ashamed of me."

"Oh, sweetheart. I'm not ashamed of you."

Delphine's head jerked up. She stared blindly past Hardwick, and he turned, still protecting her with his body, until he could see who had spoken.

It was her mother. Sara Belgrave, with her laughing housecat eyes, who must have snuck out after them on cat-quiet feet. The twins were right behind her. He'd never thought either of them capable of being quiet, but maybe there was something of their mother's cat in them after all. They were ashen-faced and creeping with guilt.

Sara reached out towards Delphine. "I'm sad because I wish you'd told me earlier. You're my daughter, Delphy. I'm meant to protect you, not the other way around. You never needed to lie to me. I will love you no matter what, just like your father would have."

"But you wouldn't have! When I told you, you were both so—so *proud* of me." Delphine's body was shaken by a sob that left her clinging to Hardwick.

He held her up, ice gripping his spine. "You were so relieved."

Grief passed over her mother's face. "When Dominic was in the hospital."

"But it started so long before that. When you got sick. Brutus had already fledged, do you remember? He was so early. We went to his First Flight. And everyone was saying I would be next, that I couldn't let any of the other younger cousins beat me at it again. But then you got sick, and I wasn't next, and the twins were just walking and it was all Dad could do to keep us all together, and I couldn't—I couldn't have been another problem on top of that."

"Delphy, you wouldn't have been a *problem*."

"Yes, I would have been. And I had to *not* be a problem. I helped with the twins. I kept out of the way at family things—and we didn't go to many, anyway, not while you were sick." Delphine's face twisted. "I heard what Grandfather and Grandmother used to say about you. That you weren't strong enough to be married into the Belgrave family. But then you got better."

"And then your father died." Sara caught Hardwick's expression of mingled horror and confusion. She steadied herself and explained: "My husband was killed in a traffic accident when Delphine was young. He—a truck came off the road and he pushed me out of the way rather than save himself."

That was what the older Belgraves had been talking about, Hardwick realized. A Belgrave sacrificing himself for family.

And they hadn't thought Sara was worth the sacrifice.

"The doctors kept him stable long enough for the children to say goodbye, but he was too injured for even his shifter healing to save him." The sadness in Sara's eyes was years old.

"He told me—" Delphine's voice choked to a stop. He focused on the mate bond and tried to send her reassurance, strength, but it was as slippery as ever and danced out of his reach. Delphine took a shaking breath. "He told me not to let anyone ever tell me there was anything wrong with me. But there was. I couldn't tell him that, so I said—I lied—I told him my lioness had come in. That I was normal. That I was a real Belgrave. And he was relieved, Mum. You both were. You'd been so worried and you were *relieved* I was normal."

"Oh, sweetheart. We knew there are no guarantees when two shifters of different types have a child. The same as there are no guarantees when a shifter and a human do."

"I'd argue there aren't any guarantees what you're going to get when two shifters with the same animal get together, either," Hardwick added in a low voice. "My folks sure didn't know what they were getting with me." A griffin shifter, the same as they were—but with a griffin who didn't speak, and who couldn't be around lies without getting a migraine.

Sara gave him a sympathetic look. "We knew Dominic's parents would make things difficult if we had a child who wasn't a winged lion shifter. We were worried because we didn't want you to face that, not because we would love you any less."

"We're not like the rest of them! We don't *care*, Delphy. We only care that you're okay. And I—" Anders' face was practically gray. "I'm sorry I told everyone your secret. I promised you I wouldn't and then the first thing I did was break that promise. I was just so *mad*. All the things he was saying, about Dad and Mum and you had to just sit there and listen to him."

"It's okay, Anders. And you too, Vance, I know if Anders hadn't said it you would have been right on his tail." Delphine took a deep breath. "It—it needed to come out, I think. And I never would have let it happen by myself." Her lips curved in a sad smile. "Now everyone knows I'm not a real Belgrave, and… maybe that's okay."

"Delphine. No." Sara's gaze was firm and loving. "We were relieved when we thought you were a shifter. I'll admit that. But we would never have treated you any differently if we had known the truth. You still would have been our daughter. You still would have been a Belgrave." Her hand closed over Delphine's. "You still are. And a Monroe, too."

Her maiden name, Hardwick guessed. Delphine shivered.

"You mean that?" she whispered.

"I mean it, Delphy. You are my daughter, and I love you, and your father would say the same if he was here today. You are part of this family. You *belong*." She straightened her shoulders. "I think we all agree now that anyone who says otherwise isn't worth talking to." The twins nodded fervently.

The hope in Delphine's eyes hurt Hardwick's heart. He opened his mouth to reassure her that her mother was telling the truth, but she raised a hand, stopping him.

"You don't need to tell me," she told him. "I know she's telling the truth."

She rushed into her mother's arms. Her brothers joined the family hug, their relief an almost solid force in the air and their voices cracking as they told Delphine that they loved her, too, and they didn't want her to hate them. Hardwick didn't need his gift to know that they were telling the truth. The tears in their voices were enough.

At last Delphine untangled herself and stepped back, wiping her eyes. "I didn't think this would ever be possible," she said. "Thank you. I love you all. But…"

"We're still exiled from the family breakfast." Anders had some of the sparkle in his eye back.

"No food, no presents, nowhere to sleep off a non-existent Christmas dinner," Vance added.

"That wasn't what I was going to say." Delphine's eyes shone as she turned to Hardwick but kept talking to the twins. "Can I make the food and presents and what on earth we're going to do that doesn't involve crossing paths with the rest of the family today your problem, you two, while I have a few minutes alone with Hardwick?"

# 29

## DELPHINE

They made their way to the center of the square. The last time she'd seen it, before she went port-hunting, the square had been lit up with activity. It was still lit up, but as for activity…

The end of a piece of tinsel came loose and glittered vaguely downwards.

It was the liveliest thing in the whole place.

For the week before Christmas, the Pine Valley plaza had been full of bubbling excitement. Happy cries had echoed alongside Christmas carols as friends caught sight of each other through the tinsel-spangled trees and had impromptu drinks under the strings of fairy lights, or dashing between shop fronts to admire the different festive displays each store had out. It had been like something out of a fairy tale, only instead of being populated by witches and trolls and princesses, Pine Valley was home to a sort of concentrated Christmas magic…

…and Christmas-obsessed dragons, and a pack of the friendliest hellhounds she'd ever heard of, and a surly newly fledged pegasus.

Really, witches wouldn't have been out of place.

They would be even less out of place now. Without the crowds of shoppers and holidaymakers, it looked smaller, and colder. Even the twinkling lights were a bit sad, with no one to twinkle on.

Beside her, Hardwick let out a relieved sigh.

She looked up at him. There was the ghost of a smile on his lips. Perfect for this Christmassy ghost town… which was perfect for him. Of course it was.

Delphine found an answering smile plucking at her own lips.

Perhaps instead of thinking of the place as abandoned, she should think of it as ready and waiting for them to find it.

Anders let out a jaw-popping yawn. "If I'm going to starve to death, I'm going to starve trying to eat *that* reindeer." He loped over to one of the life-sized reindeer models with silver bells and candy canes strung from its antlers and flung himself dramatically across its back. "There. *Dead.* Wait, are those real candy canes?"

"That's not a balanced breakfast, Anders," Sara said automatically. She scanned the nearest shopfronts. "Is that a restaurant? Oh, it's closed. But there must be something open. Vance, what about that bakery you found last year…" She pulled out her phone.

"It'll be shut by now," he said, but went with her when she tugged on his sleeve. They both wandered, so vaguely it had to be intentional, in a direction that could only be described as *away*. Anders closed his eyes, feigning death, sleep or both, with a candy cane sticking out of his mouth.

The square was quiet. Her family couldn't have been more obvious about giving her space for the few minutes alone she'd asked for.

She put her hands in her pockets and wandered further into the little grove of Christmas trees in the middle of the square. Hardwick kept pace with her. Each step she took seemed to press more heavily into the ground, until she felt as though she was about to sink into the snow under her own weight.

"How are you feeling?" he asked at last. "Ah, shit. I'm sorry. That's a stupid question."

His mouth twisted, bitter and self-critical. She couldn't tear her eyes away from it. She certainly couldn't look up into his eyes. Everything inside her, the new healed piece of her heart where her family's love lived and the painful piece he'd ripped out, was too muddled up.

When the rest of her family turned on her, she'd frozen up inside. Completely. Even her fingers had felt numb, and her senses dulled, as though she was encased in ice.

She hadn't dared to check on the glowing mate bond in her heart, to check that it was still there. Still alive, and not as dead and frozen as the rest of her.

But…

"Could be worse," she muttered.

Hardwick's chin jerked away from her. "They were lying. All of them, about everything. All that Belgrave family bullshit. Your grandfather's *why*. You know that, don't you?"

"But they weren't lying afterwards."

"No. They weren't."

The knowledge released something inside her. But not for Hardwick. The lines at the edges of his mouth deepened. He looked as bad as he did when she first met him. When, although she didn't know it, he'd just been thrown from the promise of a week's peace and recovery into a reality that promised pain no matter what choices he made. Be with her and let her hurt him, or lose her and rip his own heart out of his chest.

He growled low in his throat. "And the truth hurt you more than their lies could ever hurt me."

"Hardwick, you almost passed out last night after spending a couple of minutes with them."

He gestured with one hand. "I can handle my own problems. But not by causing more for you. I thought—you know I thought you should tell them. But the moment the truth came out and the pain stopped, when I saw the look on your face…" He shook his head.

"You wanted to save me."

"And if I'd tried to, I would have hurt you worse than any of them ever did." His shoulders slumped. "I hated it. Standing there, not doing anything. I should have been able to help you."

"You did. You got me out of there."

"Too late."

She shook her head. "Anders and Vance… they were just trying to help me, too. I never gave them that chance before. I thought I had everything under control, so I had to keep it that way. Belgraves don't need saving." She parroted her grandfather's words and made a face. "The whole bloody family needs saving. And I…"

Slowly, she reached out and threaded her fingers through his. He stiffened, then returned her embrace, his grip like a lifeline.

Delphine turned around and he turned with her until they were both looking back towards her family. Her mother and Vance had their heads together, looking at the cell phones, and Anders was doing a terrible job of pretending to be asleep. He kept darting his eyes open and shooting looks at them all.

"I have spent most of my life convinced that if Mum and my brothers knew the truth about me, then I would lose them. Now I have a real family for the first time since I was a child. It's more than I ever thought I could have out of life. But it's not all I want."

She turned to him, and his gaze on her face was warmer than the sun.

"I want you to keep wanting to help me. And I want to help you, too. I don't want us being together to be something that hurts you. And—I know I'm going to forget to tell the truth sometimes, or slip into old habits, or—maybe even if I'm angry, or upset. I don't want to be that person, but I can't promise I won't be."

She tucked her other hand under his arm, pulling him closer as she tried to find words for what she wanted to say.

Quiet settled around them. Not the silence of the world around the cabin; a smaller, cozier silence, somehow all the more precious because of the traces of other lives carrying on around them. The hint of music from a nearby building, the odd shriek of childish excitement from further away.

The air was cool, but not freezing. A world away from the icy mountainside where she'd spent the last few days with Hardwick.

She'd thought of that as *his* world and this as *her* world but that was wrong too, wasn't it?

He'd been hiding from people that caused him pain. She'd been hiding—as alone as Hardwick had been among the people who could cause her the most pain, hiding her true self to keep herself safe.

But maybe there was a place they could be safe, and themselves, together.

"I never expected to find someone like you," she said. "I thought, everything else about me that should have been magical didn't exist, so why would I have a mate anywhere in the world? And if I had imagined who my mate would be—"

"You wouldn't have imagined me."

"Not even slightly." She laughed softly and tucked her head against his chest. He rested his hand tentatively on the back of her neck and she sighed, listening to the thud of his heart through his coat.

Even this close, though, there was still distance between them. Still some ice left to thaw before she let herself look into her heart. "I would have imagined someone I had to keep the truth a secret from and keep away from my family, and I would have stayed trapped in the life I had built for myself. Even when I knew you were mine, and knew that I couldn't keep living a lie, I thought that if you met my family and they found out the truth then I would be left crawling back to you because you were all I had left in the world. I know that lying was wrong, but I couldn't see how I could live with that and not end up resenting you. But now…"

She molded herself against him, pressing her breasts against his chest, stomach to stomach, standing so close if either of them moved too quickly their legs would tangle and they would end up on the ground.

"...Now, I'm so glad I found you. I'm glad everyone knows the truth. And I know it's going to be difficult, and we have so much to learn about each other and figure out and get wrong before we get right, but I'm not scared. I have spent so long pretending to myself about what I want and don't want, and I know, right now, that what I want is to be with you."

"Delphine, I..." Hardwick crushed her to him. "I don't deserve this."

"Yes, you do. You changed my life for the better." She wriggled in his grasp just enough so she could look up at his face and brush a strand of hair away from his eyes. "You wanted to save me. I say you did. Not just today. Not just when you pulled me out of the snow. Every minute we've been together."

She kissed him. His lips were slow to respond, then urgent and hungry. She guessed—no, she *knew*—that he had been processing what she'd said, his griffin picking it over for lies. The kiss had surprised him. But now he wasn't letting her go.

He was passionate and demanding, his teeth grazing her lips and his hand firm on the back of her head. Her mind darted back to the night they'd spent together: his body hard against hers, his possessive joy at her telling him what she wanted and what she wanted being him. She'd been afraid she was asking too much. Too hard, too fast, too *obvious*. But he'd more than accepted her. He'd relished every secret desire she whispered in his ear.

And she was going to get a lifetime of that.

And of finding out his secret desires in return.

As though he was reading her mind, Hardwick broke off the kiss and muttered roughly in her ear: "You said that I'm yours."

"You are."

He made a sound that was more growl than word and kissed her again.

And deep inside her heart, light blossomed like dawn on a frosty morning.

# 30

# HARDWICK

The town's only restaurant was closed for the holiday, as were the bakeries and coffee shops. But Pine Valley had more miracles in store that Christmas.

Jasper Heartwell came roaring into the square just before lunchtime. His Range Rover was bright red, with white trim and tinsel around the windows. The horn played the first bars of the chorus of 'All I Want for Christmas'.

The twins sagged under the onslaught of uncoolness. Delphine, still tucked against Hardwick's side, raised her head in surprise. Her mother sent him a silent question and, when he confirmed who the newcomer was, smoothed her clothing self-consciously. He didn't know how to reassure her.

"Don't worry, Mum," Delphine said. She laid her head against Hardwick's shoulder and waved to the dragon shifter as he leapt out of the truck. "Jasper Heartwell has a human mate. I don't think he would—"

"Belgraves!" Jasper called. "I heard there was a Christmas crisis brewing!"

*Who told him that?* Hardwick wondered. The light in his chest throbbed and Delphine turned to him, surprise on her face.

"Did you just ask—" she began, then shook her head. "There was a snowy owl hanging around earlier. I think it might have been Olly, Jackson's mate. She must have heard—" She bit her lip.

"And she sent in the cavalry." Hardwick kissed the top of her head.

Jasper drove them up the valley towards his family homestead. The Heartwells' home was massive and solidly, reassuringly lived-in looking. Cars and trucks were parked higgledy-piggledy on the drive. Children's toboggans and skis were piled up next to the huge double front doors. Another toboggan was perilously balanced on the roof. Occasional patches of the building's log cladding were a darker shade, charred-looking.

Hardwick stared. Not just charred-looking. *Charred.*

Jasper cleared his throat. "My daughter's work," he explained. "She found her dragon very early. And flying. And fire breathing."

"She sounds like a quick learner."

"Precisely!" His eyes lit up. "And now that we've installed a few extra rain barrels, we haven't had any actual near-disasters in, oh, months."

"And during the winter you have the snow, as well," Delphine added.

"It does have an excellent dampening effect, that's true. Now…" Jasper pulled into a spare park and twisted around in his seat to look at all of his passengers. "I don't know the details of how you ended up out in the cold at Christmas, but nobody's going to bother you about it once we're inside. Heartwell Christmases are about celebrating, not prying."

Hardwick's griffin stretched out its neck, but it couldn't find a whisper of a lie in Jasper's voice, or his multi-colored eyes.

"I appreciate that," Delphine said softly.

Jasper grinned. "Then let's head inside."

Christmas at the Heartwells was not just about celebrating; it was something worth celebrating. Hardwick braced himself as he walked inside, but the only thing that hit him was a wall of heat. The conversation in the living room was closer to a roar, with a toddler in the middle of the room, surrounded by shredded wrapping paper, supplying a high-pitched shriek that cut through the rest.

People were talking. Laughing. Exclaiming over gifts, and telling stories, and a thousand other things all at once, and no one was lying.

The knots in Hardwick's shoulders eased. Inside him, his griffin relaxed, the feathers on its spine feeling out-of-place as they lay down.

Jasper started a lightning round of introductions. "Hardwick and Delphine, you've already met my sister and her husband." Opal and Hank waved from a sofa, where they were snuggled together, picking at the last scraps of buttered croissants and various cheeses. Their son was sprawled in front of the enormous, spangled Christmas tree, his head firmly in a book. "Cole you know, and this is my mate, Abigail—" A short, plump woman looked up from where she was sitting on the floor with the toddler, and Hardwick saw only humanity in her eyes. "—and my daughter, Ruby—"

"The fire-starter?" Hardwick asked in an undertone.

Jasper laughed. "My little firebug! I mean—no—not now, sweetheart…"

The adorable toddler disappeared. In her place, a ruby-scaled dragonling crouched in a nest of wrapping paper. She eyed the flammable stuff with keen interest.

Abigail made a warning sound, and Jasper swooped in and grabbed their daughter as smoke started to pour from the dragonling's nostrils. He ran out the French windows leading outside just as she let out a tiny burp of flame.

Abigail stood up. "Welcome to the madhouse," she said, smiling at them all. "I'd say this hardly ever happens, but I'm not sure there's any point. Have you had breakfast yet?"

"Abigail! The emergency presents!" Jasper called from the yard, where Ruby was doing her best to set fire to a snowman.

"Breakfast first!" she called back. She raised her eyebrows at her guests—the twins in particular. "Yes?"

They agreed, loudly and at length, until their mouths were too full of pastry to keep talking.

Conversation swelled around him, filling the house with warmth and joy. It turned out that his old colleague Jackson's mate Olly had been hanging around in owl form ever since she saw the twins climbing down the outside of the hotel earlier that morning. She'd wanted to know what the hell was going on, and when she put it all together, she'd told Jackson and they'd alerted the Heartwells.

The Heartwells were as different from the Belgraves as it was possible to be. Different from the wider Belgrave clan, that was. This small offshoot, Delphine and the people who loved her, were a fierce knot of love that burned all the brighter for how close it had come to being lost forever. Hardwick would have pushed through any amount of pain for that.

But there was no pain.

Even when Opal rounded up Cole to help in the kitchen, he didn't try to bluff his way out of it. He complained, but even his teenaged whining didn't contain any actual lies. "But I want to read my book," he said, and "Can't we just eat more croissants?" and "But it's not *fair*!"

"Would you rather go outside and look after Ruby so your uncle can help?"

"*Ughhhhhhh.*" Cole kicked his feet but followed his mother out of the living room.

Hardwick's griffin sifted through each sentence, pulling the words to pieces and flipping the pieces over with its beak. It couldn't find so much as a trace of untruth. For whatever reason, objective reality agreed that it *wasn't* fair that Cole had to help set up for lunch. Maybe his parents had told him he could have Christmas off chores; maybe growing up and having to drag your nose out of a good book in order to help out just plain *wasn't* fair. Maybe living in the same house as an arsonist toddler meant 'fairness' was left by the wayside long ago.

Delphine caught his eye and left the room. Assuming she was heading for the kitchen to re-enact the Cinderella role she used to play with her own family, Hardwick followed her—and found her waiting for him in a quiet alcove.

She slipped her hands around his waist and drew him closer to her. He went to her without resisting. Outside, their touches had been muffled by the thick layers of their winter clothing; now, there was only a thin layer of knit fabric between his hands and her warm, inviting skin.

And a similar, solitary layer of cotton between her fingers and his skin. She untucked his shirt with a matter-of-fact swiftness that made his heart soar. Despite what he had done, Delphine still claimed him as hers. Her hands sliding up his back left no doubt about that.

Then she kissed him, and his thoughts splintered into blinding light.

The splinters of light rushed to fill his veins, then pulled back until there was only that single burning sun inside his heart. Stronger and brighter than before, and the thread connecting him to Delphine was more like a plaited rope.

Delphine pulled away so slowly that somehow the act of ending the kiss was more charged than the kiss itself had been. Her amber eyes bored into his, pupils huge and dark.

"Um," she said, sounding as stunned as he felt. "That's not what I came out here to do, but it's…"

She kissed him again and gasped as the light connecting them pulsed.

"It's stronger," she breathed against his lips.

He waited for her to say *isn't it?* and for self-doubt to darken her sparkling eyes. But she didn't. Instead, her smile filled his heart.

"What do you think makes it change?" she asked, and the answer was on his lips before he'd even thought about it.

"Wanting it to be true," he said. "Accepting that it's real. That we might be good together, after all."

"Oh, might we?" Her smile turned teasing. "Is that the truth?"

He answered her with a kiss that turned urgent too quickly.

Neither of them wanted to pull away, but the sound of a door closing made them jump away from each other guiltily.

"We'd better not," Delphine murmured, her cheeks flushed.

Heat coiled between them. "Better not what?"

Whatever Delphine saw in his eyes, it made her tip her head back, part teasing, part defiant. "Disappear into a spare room somewhere and abandon our hosts who've so kindly taken us in on Christmas Day?"

"Sounds good to me."

"Hardwick!"

He felt drunk. Not just on desire, though that was a part of it. A weighty, wanting part of it. But it was happiness, too. Happiness so intense it made him light-headed.

"Don't you want to test my theory?"

"What theory?"

"About this." He kissed her again, long and slow, and the golden light that connected them glowed like a sunrise. "You remember when it first appeared, don't you?"

Delphine made a soft, breathy noise against his lips that was better than a *yes*. Her fingers clutched in his hair.

They'd both felt the connection from the moment they first laid eyes on each other. But it wasn't until they'd slept together that the light of the mate bond had started to flicker in their hearts.

"We could talk to the Heartwells," she said. "Do some background research. Find out how they experienced the beginning of their mate bonds, compare what we're feeling—"

"Don't you dare," he growled, and Delphine pressed her face into the crook of his neck and laughed.

"No," she agreed. "I'm sick of looking to other people to know how I should behave and experience things. I want to find out for myself. With you."

His griffin crooned.

"Now?" he suggested.

Delphine half-groaned, half-laughed into his shoulder but before he could decide whether he was joking or not and, bad manners or not, the scales were weighting towards not, a door opened and the swell of conversation rushed out towards them.

"I've got my eyes closed!" one of Delphine's brothers called. "'Cos I don't want to see whatever's going on out here." Laughter from the other room. "Lunch is ready, if you two want to get in before it all vanishes—"

"Or move further away!" someone else called. Delphine choked, her cheeks burning.

"Caught," she muttered, and reluctantly unwound herself from his arms. "We'd better go in. No, wait…"

He waited while she thought, her bottom lip lightly caught between her teeth.

"Not *we'd better*," she said after a moment. "But *let's*. I haven't had a good Christmas with my family in so long, and…" She stood on tiptoes to whisper into his ear. "…we still have the rest of the day to experiment with your theory. If that's what we're calling it."

With that promise burning in his ear, Hardwick had to force himself to let her go and tidy his own clothes before they rejoined the others. Just before they reached the door, he hooked one arm around her waist and asked:

"What did you come out here for in the first place?"

"Before you distracted me?" Her teeth flashed in a smile, but her eyes were gentle. "I wanted to check on you. I didn't think you'd want me to ask in front of everyone. How are you feeling?"

She pressed the back of one hand against his forehead. He took it and kissed it, trailing his lips across her fingertips. "How do you think?"

Her eyes narrowed. "Good enough to tease me about it, clearly."

"I feel—" *fine,* he'd been about to say, before his griffin's claws pricked warningly at him. "—better than I expected."

"But still not fully healed."

"It's easier around the Heartwells. They don't have any reason to lie in their own home, I guess."

"Unlike my family." Her eyes shadowed.

He tipped her head back until he could meet her gaze. "Your family here is fine, Delphine. They're not hurting me."

"Good." There was more than just care for him in her eyes. The relieved love she had for her small, healed family washed over him… through the mate bond.

Hardwick closed his eyes and let it sink in. Then he returned what he was feeling, tentatively winding the emotions around the golden light that connected them.

Love. Ease. So much happiness he thought he might burst. And a determination that Delphine should have the Christmas she so badly deserved.

Delphine gasped. "Was that—?"

"Yes."

Someone called them for lunch again, but they stayed where they were, sinking into one another's eyes.

The same someone, or another one, knocked on the door. "You'll miss out on the ham if you wait any longer!" they called.

"And the potatoes!"

"And the roast goose!"

Delphine shook herself. "Not fully healed," she said vaguely, as though coming out of a dream. "You need to eat."

He couldn't argue with that.

"And after that…" She kissed him lightly. "We'll need some time on our own, won't we, for you to heal properly? Another retreat."

"Together."

"Together," she agreed.

The day had more surprises in store for them. After the meal, Jasper made good on his promise (or threat) of emergency presents. He had a store of them, apparently, kept safe in the attic for Christmas crises. Hardwick found himself the proud new owner of a Christmas sweater featuring a red-nosed husky dog. The twins whooped over matching toboggans as though they were Cole's age, not freshmen. And Delphine unwrapped a stack of books that made her double over with laughter. He didn't understand until she tilted the covers towards them.

They were the same series of airport thrillers that she'd so completely failed to read up in the cabin.

"Maybe you'll have better luck getting into them this time," he deadpanned.

Delphine gulped back another burst of laughter and wiped her eyes. "I hope not."

There was more food after the presents. The teenagers all headed out to cause trouble in the snow, laden down with their new toys and bags of candy, while the adults and a miraculously dozing toddler settled down in the living room.

And then the first extra visitor arrived.

Hardwick's griffin was on alert from the first whisper of wings outside. Jasper and Hank were already looking up when he glimpsed golden eagle wings at the corner of the window and, a few minutes later, heard a knock on the door.

They all exchanged a look. Sara sighed and smoothed down her skirt. "I know who that is," she said carefully. "I'll go and ask what they—"

"Absolutely not!" Jasper declared. He leapt to his feet and was blocking the living room door before she could even move. "You're our guests. I'll let them in."

It was one of Delphine's cousins—the older one with the Flintstones name.

"Pebbles!" Delphine exclaimed. "What are you doing here?"

Her mate was with her. They both looked nervously around as Delphine's mother made quick introductions. Then Pebbles burst out:

"We couldn't stay there any longer! It's awful. Grandmother and Grandfather said—"

Her mate's expression pinched and Hardwick sensed the strange mental whisper of private telepathic chatter. Pebbles' chin went up.

"You're right. That's family business." Her expression settled. "Auntie Sara, Delphine, we want you to know that we've decided—"

Hardwick braced himself. He'd guessed that the revelation that the Belgrave line didn't run 'true' with Delphine might cause problems for Pebbles and her bird of paradise mate, but however panicked they were now, he didn't trust them not to twist lies around their words.

"Wait." Delphine stood up and moved in front of her cousin. Between them and him, Hardwick realized. "Before you say anything, you have to know that Hardwick can sense it when you lie."

Calculations flashed behind Pebbles' eyes. "Oh, that's—"

"And it hurts him." Delphine's voice flattened. "And if you hurt him, I'll throw you out of here, family or not."

Hardwick's heart filled. His mate was protecting him. From her family—the same family that, a day ago, she would have thrown herself into traffic to appease.

But not him. The light in his chest flared, and the emotion that flowed through it from his mate was as good as a word: *Mine.*

He was hers. And the same as she was protecting him, he would make sure she found the confidence and trust in herself to defend herself as much as she was defending him.

"Oh, er, that's…" Pebbles looked lost. Her mate took her hand.

"Tell them, then," he said.

Pebbles drew herself up. "It's chaos down there," she admitted. "Everyone's fighting. You just *left*. And I thought—it wasn't fair, how they abandoned…"

Hardwick sucked in a breath. It wasn't a full lie, but it was close enough.

Delphine actually *growled.*

"I mean—I mean they started looking at us, too, and Grandmother asked if we were *sure* we wanted to have children, and how she understood that young people these days sometimes wanted to have c-careers instead, or travel, and that if that was what we wanted then it would be *just fine with her.*" Her face went blotchy, red vivid against white. "They're not even mates! They've been pretending all this time that Belgraves are so, so *blessed*, and the truth is it's all a lie, it's all *fake*. She said we shouldn't…"

Her voice wavered out and she buried her face in her mate's shoulder. He stared at the rest of them, his gaze defiant, and Hardwick wondered how much it had taken from the other man over the years to be a part of the Belgrave clan, surrounded by their cultish self-absorption.

Delphine had wanted to spare him that. The day by day, week by week wearing away of his own beliefs and wants and hopes against the driving force of Belgrave selfishness.

"So, we are here now," Pascal said. "Not as fast as you, though."

"Did they throw you out?" Delphine asked, her voice tight.

He shrugged, but there was a tension in the movement that made Pebbles raise her head and brush his hair off his face. "The party atmosphere was not so great by then, anyway."

"And you've come here to—"

Pebbles replied. "Apolo—no. Shouldn't lie." Her mouth twisted. "You were so brave, leaving like you did. I don't feel brave. I feel like I've been so stupid, and I should have seen so much earlier... including you. We practically grew up together, Delphy, and I never saw..."

"I never wanted you to."

She drew in a ragged breath. "Grandfather said that you're the one I should be angry at. Because you hid the truth and if I'd known earlier that you weren't a winged lion shifter, I would have made better choices. As though Pascal isn't the best choice I made in my life!"

"We brought our bags. And your luggage, too." A nervous smile. "I do not particularly wish to go back to that hotel, but if you are finding other accommodations, perhaps we could..."

"Join the party!" Jasper suggested, clapping his hands together. "Er—if that's all right with our other guests, of course."

Delphine hesitated. Her indecision fluttered down the mate bond—and then her certainty, bright as the midday sun. "Of course," she said. "They are family, after all. Real family."

Pebbles and Pascal weren't the only Belgraves to slink through the Heartwells' door. The other younger cousins appeared mid-afternoon, bedraggled and beaten down, and Jasper was merrily run off his feet trying to find places for them all to stay. They all had the same story: that once Delphine left, the Belgrave clan had started to splinter, revealing cracks that ran so deep nothing could keep it together.

Hardwick took Delphine aside during a quiet moment, to check that she was alright.

She looked dazed. "I think I am," she said softly, watching Brutus and Livia help Ruby build a snow-lion in the yard. "I... I don't know. I should feel awful, but I don't. I did what I always feared. Tore my family apart."

He waited, and after a few moments, she lifted her chin and looked him in the eyes.

"But I *don't* feel awful. I feel like if all it took for my grandparents to lose control of the family was me leaving before they could cast me aside, then they deserve to watch it all fall apart."

The sudden growl in her voice went straight to his heart. He pulled her to him, kissing her until they were both breathless. "Good," he rumbled against her lips.

"Thank you."

"For what?"

Her lips curved against his. "My Christmas present."

His heart almost stopped. He hadn't gotten her anything. No matter than he hadn't known she existed until a few days ago, and there hadn't exactly been time to go shopping. "I didn't—"

"You did." She nuzzled against him. "Because of you, I get to figure out who I really am, when I'm not trying to be something I'm not. And I get to do that *with* you. That's the best Christmas present I could ever imagine."

They slipped into the shadows. It was almost dinner time; any minute now, someone would come hunting for them. This time, though, he wasn't sure they would go.

Delphine's eyes shone in the dying light. "You're looking happy," she said.

"So are you."

She smiled, and the glow in his chest lit up. The light that had kindled first as a weak, flickering thing flared like a bonfire. "I wonder why that might be."

"No, you don't."

"No," she agreed, reaching up to kiss him again. "I don't."

# 31

## DELPHINE

Hardwick's scent filled her mind as he pushed her against the wall. Wild, passionate, and *hers*.

He gasped against her lips. "Do that again."

*Mine.*

The feeling darted down the mate bond, sharp and greedy and unashamed. Hardwick moaned.

"And you're mine." His voice sent lightning down her spine and made heat unfurl between her legs.

The Heartwells had offered them their guesthouse for the night. Opal had called it 'that little cabin down by the edge of the property,' but that hardly did it justice. Not after the 'little cabin' she and Hardwick had spent their first few nights together in.

Honeymoon suite, more like.

The small house was tucked away privately, out of sight of the main lodge. Its décor was all solid wood and thick pillows and infinitely fall-upon-able. She and Hardwick hadn't bothered unpacking the luggage that Pebbles and Pascal had smuggled up.

The teasing desire that had built almost to breaking point as they laughed and talked and celebrated with the Heartwells and the newly forged, smaller Belgrave clan had lasted until they closed the door behind them and then shattered. Spectacularly.

She knew Hardwick hadn't packed many shirts. That didn't stop her from ripping his off.

His chest was hot under her fingers, his heartbeat a drum that echoed in her own chest. She kissed his collarbone, his pecs, ran greedy fingers down the planes of his abs and hooked them into his belt. He growled something that was all meaning and no words, his own fingers slipping as he tried to pull off her own shirt. She teased him, drawing the belt through its buckle oh-so-slowly, and he swore deep in his throat.

"Please," he begged, and she let him go, stepped back, raised her arms obediently for him to strip her.

He was more controlled than she was. He dropped to his knees in front of her, raising the hem of her sweater inch by inch and peppering her bare skin with kisses. Every touch made every other inch of her skin want to be touched. By the time he reached her breasts, she was shaking.

This was so much more intense than the first time they'd had sex. That had been all fierce need, lust mingling with frustration and the half-wonder, half-terror of knowing the connection she'd sensed was real. Now, Hardwick's mouth on her was like a blessing, sweet and longing.

He dropped her sweater on the floor and pulled down the straps of her bra one at a time, caressing the soft skin of her breasts and touching his lips to her nipples. Goosebumps prickled across her skin. She gasped, arching her back, her whole body singing out more, more.

"Please, I want you to—" Her breath hitched as he circled her nipple with his tongue. "—teeth—"

He bit down, gently, and Delphine's legs almost gave out. Only Hardwick's strong hands around her waist kept her upright. And he kept biting, light, teasing brushes of tooth against skin, up her neck, to her heat-washed lips.

There was a question in his eyes. "What is it?" she asked.

"Last time…" His hands ghosted down her sides. She hitched her hips towards him, and he moaned as her stomach pressed against the hardness between his legs. "It was incredible. If you want to do that again—"

"I want," she murmured, raising one finger to outline his lips, "whatever you want."

His pupils darkened. "Slower?"

"Slower."

"God, I love you."

Love. The word dove home in Delphine's chest, piercing her heart. She was helpless as he kissed her again, as slowly as he'd asked for, his fingers slipping under her waistline and pushing her trousers down. Slowly, slowly. She would want fast and hard again, she knew, but this, now, was perfect.

He teased her until she thought she would go mad. She was slick with need, hot and loose-limbed with want. When she slid down his body, laying kisses in a trail that went from his neck to his stomach, his arms tightened around her as though he thought she really was falling. She gently pushed his hands away and sank lower.

He groaned as she pulled at his belt again—slowly, slowly—and she relished the sound. When she freed his cock at last a thrill pulsed between her legs.

She kissed the end of it first, then along one side. Hardwick's hands tangled in her hair. "Oh, God, Delphine—"

His hips twitched as she wrapped her lips around his tip and she drew back, a smile hovering around her mouth. "Who said he wanted 'slower'?" she reminded him.

The expression in his eyes made her breath catch.

She held his gaze as she put her mouth on him again, sucking his cock in with sensual, excruciating slowness. She tasted a hint of salt as she swirled her tongue across the head of his cock and felt

Hardwick's groan thrum against her lips. Her own hum, pleasurable and low, made him twitch against her.

When she thought they were both about to break, she pulled away and rose to her feet again. Hardwick crushed her to his chest, his breathing ragged. They made their way to the bedroom, feet tripping over themselves, every step an excuse to stop and kiss and run hungry hands over one another. At last, Hardwick picked her up and lowered her gently onto a coverlet that was soft as a cloud beneath her back. He eased her pants off and stood back, his dark eyes hooded as he stared at her.

"You're beautiful," he said, his voice honey mixed with gravel.

There was no self-consciousness. Delphine glowed beneath his hot gaze, basking in his admiration. How could she be self-conscious about being this man's mate?

"And I'm yours." Her voice was husky.

He lowered himself over her with the grace of a predatory animal, his lean muscles hardly hinting at his strength. When his skin touched hers, she gasped. He was all heat, all desire and passion and perfect, possessive want.

She opened her legs and he pushed himself inside her. Last time, his brutal pace had left her breathless; this time, her chest was tight with wonder. Every sensation was amplified, from the stretch of his thick length to the whispers of love he breathed into her ear. She angled her hips, welcoming him in, wanting him to fill her completely. When he finally hilted himself completely it was so perfect, she thought she would break apart.

Then he rocked his hips against hers, and she saw stars.

She clenched around him, slowness impossible now, her orgasm a rolling, storm-whipped ocean of peaks that grew higher and higher. Arms outflung, she was barely aware of her cries until Hardwick muffled them with a kiss. She wrapped her legs around his hips so that next time he pulled out she stayed with him, locked in place, her hips lifted off the bed, and when he thrust down again he drove another storm of pleasure through her.

She was limp and exhausted by the time he came, one hand gripping her hip with bruising strength and the other knotted in her hair. He kissed her, pleasure a growl on his lips as his cock pulsed.

"I love you," she whispered, all other words beyond her.

"And I you." He raised his head. She sank into his dark eyes, just looking at him. Why not? There was no need for words. She'd already drowned in pleasure, and he knew that she was his. Just like he was *hers*.

The mate bond suddenly burst into brilliant light. She'd likened it to a sun before; now it was as though she was *in* the sun, her whole body filled with white-gold light. Hardwick exclaimed in wonder. He pressed his forehead against hers, and the sheer strength of the love that poured through the mate bond into her heart overwhelmed her.

*Yes,* she thought, *yes, like this, forever. This is what I want.* She sent that feeling through the mate bond to his heart, too, and his joy was a spring chorus in her soul.

The light faded, but her whole body felt light, as though it was feeling an after-image of the mate bond's magical power. Hardwick rolled over and gathered her to him.

"Happy Christmas," he murmured to her.

"The first of many," she promised him.

And it was the truth.

# EPILOGUE
## DELPHINE

Hardwick dropped a crate on the kitchen table and brushed off his hands. "That's the last of them."

Delphine resisted the urge to dust off the rest of him, too. He'd managed to keep his clothes on the first few times he shifted, but they had enough luggage that the last few trips, he either hadn't managed it or hadn't bothered.

Hardwick caught her admiring glance and raised one eyebrow.

*Why am I resisting the urge?* she asked herself and sauntered over to carefully brush quickly melting snowflakes off his broad shoulders.

"Enough to last us through the end of January." She put her arms around his waist and surveyed the kitchen. There were another half-dozen wooden crates brimming with groceries on the table, not including the perishables she'd already begun storing in the fridge and chest freezer. Hardwick might have been happy living off frozen pizza alone when he tried this the first time, but a girl needed her gooey cheeses, damn it.

The Heartwells had been over the moon when she and Hardwick said they needed a place to stay—and that the old cabin Hardwick had rented for Christmas just wasn't going to cut it without an emergency roof replacement. Opal and Jasper had pored over their property listings with so much glee that Delphine was left wondering whether the dragon siblings hoarded gold, like all the stories said, or vacation homes.

After ruling out houses that were too close to town, too close to the winter sledding tracks, or otherwise unsuitable for reasons that seemed perfectly clear to the Heartwells but mystified Delphine, they had settled on a rustic one-bedroom cottage that was so far off the beaten track you had to fly in. Hardwick had flown Delphine in first, with the key, and then made as many trips as it took to bring in all their gear.

They'd had plenty of offers of help, of course; every flying shifter in the valley had volunteered to help ferry bags and boxed, but Hardwick had declined. Delphine was glad about that. It meant that this time together started the way it was meant to go on: just them.

She leaned against him, as though she was trying to warm him up and not the other way around.

There was no doubt left in her mind that they were mates, and meant to be together—but 'meant to be together' in the long run and 'meant to be together right now' weren't necessarily the same thing.

"A whole month," she said. "I've still got the car keys if you decide you need the time actually alone."

Hardwick stiffened in her arms. "Why would you say that?"

*Because*—She bit her lip and forced herself not to weave a make-nice story. Hardwick was watching her, a familiar, hard wariness in his eyes. "Because you're still exhausted and you're still hurting more than you should when people lie, and I—I don't know how good I'll be at not lying. I'll do my best. But I don't want to slip up and hurt you." She raised one hand to rest against his cheek.

He didn't rush to reassure her. That was reassuring in of itself. He was taking her seriously. And taking his own health seriously.

"You don't hurt me anymore," he said, covering her hand with his.

She swallowed. "You don't have to—"

"Delphine. Do I lie?"

Delphine stared into her mate's dark eyes. "No, you don't, but..." Self-consciousness was an itch beneath her skin. "If you're trying to save my feelings—I know that just being around me gave you

a headache, when we first met. You don't have to…
to…"

His steady, loving gaze didn't change.

"Oh," she whispered. "You're not trying to save
my feelings. You're telling the truth."

"I always will be." He tightened his fingers around
hers and turned his head to kiss the palm of her hand.
"You can count on that. I'll always tell you the truth
and right now, and forever, the truth is that you only
hurt me when you were afraid. I didn't see that as fast
as I could have. You were afraid of what your family
would think, what they'd do, if they knew the truth.
You built this whole idea of yourself around those
lies, and that was what hurt me. But that's in the
past now." He kissed each of her fingers, one by one.
"This month isn't just about me. I want you to have a
chance to learn who you can be, too. Underneath all
the stories you told yourself. And figuring that out
won't be lying. It'll be discovering your truth."

Tears filled her eyes. He understood her? He
understood her, and still wanted her around?

Hardwick pulled her closer and wiped the corner
of her eye where a tear threatened to spill out. "We're
in this together, Delphine. I'm not going to push you
away."

To her horror, she sniffed. "Oh, God," she
muttered, pulling away to wipe her eyes. He didn't
let her, and she stayed safe in his arms as he kissed her

tears away. "You wouldn't have to push me away. I'd go by myself."

"I know. But I don't want that. I don't want you to ever think you have to leave for my own good." He rested his forehead against hers. "You're the best thing in my life, Delphine. Where you go, I go."

His words echoed in her mind. She didn't know whether she wanted to capture them under glass and keep them safe and perfect forever, or let them sink into her memory and know they would pop up by themselves in the future, tiny blessings that would make her day happier.

For the time being, they reminded her of something else that she had barely let herself think about. But if he wanted to stay with her, no matter what…

"I was thinking…"

She hesitated as her mind ran ahead.

Hardwick nudged her. "Go on."

"What?"

"Whatever it is that you're thinking." He rubbed a callused thumb along her arm, just above her elbow. She couldn't feel the scratch through her sweater, but she wanted to.

That probably wasn't what he was talking about, though.

"It won't hurt you if I talk through things without thinking them over first, to make sure they're actually true?"

"Try me."

She narrowed her eyes at him. She didn't want to *try him*. The whole *point* of being out here was that nobody *tried him*, and he got *better*.

She told him as much, and he laughed, surprised.

"No lies there." He tucked a strand of hair behind her air. "Now try again."

"Fine." After all, she'd already checked the—

Delphine caught herself. "I've already checked the bedroom, and the bed's made, so if this turns out to be the terrible idea I think it is, you can lie down in there until your headache goes away."

"That's not going to be a problem. Though I can think of another use for the bed." He looked so pleased with himself that she *tsk*ed at him.

"I was thinking that, yes, I do have a job that I need to get back to, but… Mr. Petrakis's good-karma kick seems to still be holding strong, so he might think that letting me have unlimited time off while he gets fitted for his halo is a good idea, and even if he doesn't to start with I could probably talk him around to thinking it was his idea in the first place…"

"Just make sure I'm out of earshot when you do that part."

She peers up at him, searching his face for the hitch. "You're okay with me talking about misleading someone else?"

"At least you're being honest about it." He gives her a crooked smile. "And I should be honest with you, too. You're not the only one who's been thinking. I'm leaving the force."

"What?"

She stepped back, to get a better view of his face and try to decide if he was joking. He couldn't be lying, but—joking, surely. "After everything you've said about how your gift makes you the perfect detective?"

"At the cost of my health, and my griffin's health." He ran one hand down his face. "I thought I was doing fine. I told myself I was enough times it's a miracle I didn't bench myself from the moment I woke up each day." He winced and she rushed forwards to place a hand on his temple. "Maybe I did. Maybe it all mixed up together, being around people when they're busy lying to save their skins or scapegoat someone else's, lying to myself…" He shook his head, then leaned into her caress. "It used to work. Do the job for eleven months and three weeks, then a few days off and I'd be back with a spring in my step and none the worse for wear. Then I needed a week, then I told myself I didn't need any more than a week and kept that up for a few years and see where it got me."

His face twisted. If it was a smile, it was a wry one. Delphine ran her fingertips along his forehead. "Nowhere good?" she suggested.

"Until you. And I was so far gone I almost let you go. No. I almost drove you away. I won't let anything like that come between us again. And thanks to you, I've found another way to use my gift to help people. Without putting myself at risk." He took her hand and his voice softened. "People who are frightened, or in danger, are always going to lie to themselves. Sometimes it's the only thing that lets them keep going."

Delphine frowned, trying to unravel what he was on the verge of telling her. "Like with the dragonling, Cole?"

"Search and rescue." He sounded gruff. He was embarrassed, Delphine realized, or—not quite, but close. Like he was waiting for her reaction before he decided this was a good idea or not. She'd been on the other side of that particular equation so many times that her heart squeezed for him. "I talked to Jackson about it. He and the hellhounds do some, but it's not any of their primary jobs. And apart from being able to shift and fly, or shift and run, they're limited in what they can do. Even the hellhounds wouldn't have been able to scent Cole's route after the snowstorm. My griffin can fly, smell and look for trails… and tell when someone's trying to tell themselves that they're not in trouble."

"And if they want to keep lying about what they were up to once you've brought them back into the warm, you can always disappear into the night, instead of sticking around to interrogate them and choke yourself on paperwork." Warmth filled her. "I think it's a great idea."

"You do?"

"You tell me."

He gave her a look that was half-proud and more than half over the border into smug. "You do."

She couldn't stop herself from prying into details. "Here? I mean, you're planning to stay in Pine Valley?"

"For the time being. If you need to be somewhere else, I'll go there. But I'm not going to drag you back into my old life."

"I'm not sure I want to drag you into mine," she admitted.

Hardwick frowned. "Your boss doesn't know the truth about you."

"And the moment he does, it'll be all 'I always knew!' and 'If only I had been there with you, to protect you from your family's wrath!' and 'I, of course, would never think less of anyone for not being a shifter!'" She made a face. "I couldn't stand it. And neither would you."

"You need to surround yourself with better people," Hardwick said grimly.

She tipped her head back to smile at him. "I'm working on it," she said. "Starting with you. And if you're thinking of staying here in Pine Valley... well, the other shifters I've met here seem to have their heads on straighter than I'm used to. Maybe they'll be a good influence on me."

"On us both," Hardwick muttered.

She gazed into his eyes. A final knot deep inside her finally started to loosen.

"This is going to work, isn't it?" she whispered. "I think I didn't actually believe it until now."

A hint of sadness flickered in the depths of his eyes, replaced quickly with warmth and love. "I'd be surprised if you let yourself fall all in, all at once."

"But I believe it now."

A slow smile spread across his face. Real happiness, because she was really telling the truth. And because—she guessed, but it was an educated guess—he'd been feeling the same way. Tentative, unsure, still feeling his way towards letting himself be open to her, just as she'd held back until she knew how he felt.

Love wasn't a one-off thing. It wasn't the universe smacking you around the head and tying you to someone. Even soulmate love. It was a dance, a series of steps, of trust given and received. They could each have chosen to pull away. But they were together. *Choosing* each other. And the connection that had sparked between them in the run-down cabin that night was nothing compared to what they would build together.

Starting now. Because he might not be acting like it, but Delphine couldn't keep distracting herself from the fact that her mate was very, very naked.

She let her eyes drop down his body and linger over some certain places so that he would have no doubts about the direction her mind was going in, and said:

"I can't make any promises that I won't lie to you by mistake, or from forgetting myself."

"I know."

"So maybe we should start with the first thing that really worked between us, for making me tell the truth."

A spark lit in his eye. "Oh?"

"I think you know what I'm talking about." Just in case he didn't, she stood on tip-toe and whispered in his ear.

His hands tightened around her waist as she went into more detail.

"... and like I said. The bed's already made. We might as well test it out."

Hardwick's eyes flashed dark fire at her. "Who says we'll make it as far as the bed?"

## HARDWICK

They did make it to the bed, eventually. But he put up a good enough fight that it took them a while.

A foggy combination of exhaustion and satisfaction filled his veins as he lay back, Delphine resting in his arms. That had been…

He searched for fancier words and came up blank. It had been everything their first time had been, but better. Then, he'd let his guard down, let himself hope that everything would be fixed between them. The sense of peace that had given him had come crashing down the next day when Delphine was reunited with her family, and maybe it was that resolution that made the memory bittersweet and what he was feeling now so much brighter.

Or maybe it was because of that first time that every time they slept together since had been so much sweeter. He'd already faced what happened when things went wrong. This time, neither of them wanted to hide anything from the other; if tomorrow morning brought on hurt, then they would face it together.

He let his eyes half-close, still looking down at Delphine tucked against his chest. He was more than just exhausted. His head felt clear, unburdened. When he checked in with his griffin, it felt the same. The constant, pained vigilance that had kept it on-edge so long that it had stopped noticing anything was wrong had eased.

When he thought of what might have been, if he'd let his own fear and pain take him away from this incredible woman, his heart quaked. It would have been less than half of a life. A shadow existence, alone, trapped in a pattern of hurt.

Instead, what lay ahead was a brighter future than had beckoned to him any other time he'd locked himself away to detox from the world.

Hell. Maybe this time next year, he'd be as keen to celebrate Christmas as Jasper Heartwell was.

# MORE PARANORMAL ROMANCE BY ZOE CHANT

## A Mate for Christmas

A Mate for the Christmas Dragon
Christmas Hellhound
Christmas Pegasus
The Hellhound's UnChristmas Miracle
Christmas Griffin

A  Gift for the Christmas Dragon (novella)

## Shifter Suspense

Claimed by the Panther
Saved by the Billionaire Lion Shifter
Stealing the Snow Leopard's Heart
Craving the Kraken
Falling for the Shadow Dragon
Seducing the Soul-Eater

# Hideaway Cove

The Griffin's Mate
The Sea Wolf's Mate
The Lightning Dragon's Mate
The Duskfire Dragon's Mate
The Kelpie's Mate

# Standalone books not in series

Her Purr-fect Christmas Mate
Trusting the Tiger
Bear With Me

# Monster Romance
# by Marie Cardno

## The Monster Girlfriend series

How to Get a Girlfriend (When You're a Terrifying Monster)
How to Get a Date with the Evil Queen
How to Get the Girl (And Not Destroy the World)

www.ingramcontent.com/pod-product-compliance
Lightning Source LLC
Chambersburg PA
CBHW020328120726
47904CB00002B/330